Erik & Isabelle

Sophomore Year
at Foresthill High

Erik & Isabelle

Sophomore Year
at Foresthill High

Kim Wallace

Sacramento

Cover design by Jon Snellstrom.

Author photo by Mark Gebhardt.

ISBN 0-9755848-1-2

Ordering information: www.foglightpress.com

Acknowledgements
&
Dedication

Thank you to all the teachers who have molded my life by their words, their lessons, and their belief that every voice matters. You have instilled in me a sense that true education extends beyond the classroom and into the world around me.

Thank you to all that have been...

My teachers of ingenuity,
My teachers of inspiration,
My teachers of imagination.

You have made a mark on my life, indelible in impact, immeasurable in effect.

Thank you to all that will be...

My teachers of
heart,
spirit,
and life.

Chapter One

"It's a boot-i-ful day in the neighborhood," Isabelle sang the Mr. Rogers theme song as she sprouted her arms through an argyle cardigan and skipped towards the nature walk. The crowd in front of her parted like the Red Sea, suggesting that her last year's reputation had not faded in her classmates' memories.

Some whispered, "Did you hear how she totally scammed on poor Mandy?" as she pranced by, while others expressed their disgust right out loud: "That chick is a sicko."

Isabelle changed her tune to "We Are Family" and discoed her way over to Erik, sticking her middle finger up at the people she left in her wake.

"Starting your year off by making some new friends, I see," Erik greeted Isabelle, as she climbed onto a boulder adjacent to his.

"School's school—pretty much the same as always." She shrugged and plopped her backpack onto the dirt.

"Call me corny, but I just love the first day of school," Erik said. "It always feels perfect."

"Yeah, whatever you say." Isabelle smirked.

Isabelle's smirk turned into a smile when she caught an approaching Maxine out of the corner of her eye. "Look, it's one of my two favorite people." She patted a sliver of space next to her and scooted over. Maxine's thigh brushed hers as she sat down, causing both girls to flinch.

Erik filed the interaction into his short-term memory. He had a hard time believing that they'd remained platonic after being inseparable all summer long. "Hi Max. How's your day so far?"

"*Perfect*?" Isabelle offered.

"Getting better every minute," she replied. "Hey, where's Salvador? I haven't seen him yet today." Maxine scouted the area.

"He went to Guatemala this summer and never came back. I got a postcard from him about a month ago," Erik replied. "That's all I heard from him."

"Is he staying there for good?" Maxine asked.

"I don't know. He didn't say. Bummer, huh?"

"That sucks. I liked Sal. He was cool."

"Yeah, we definitely have a deficit of cool people at this school," Isabelle noted, looking over at a cluster of students squealing and hugging as if they hadn't spent the entire summer together. In the middle stood Mandy Jenkins.

From another direction, they heard peals of laughter. "Poor freshman," Maxine said.

Erik peered toward the edge of the quad where a couple of sophomores were dangling a piece of freshman meat over a trash can. The kid struggled and pleaded to be let down, but no one seemed to blink an eye as they strolled by. "I hate that tradition," Erik said.

"The school promotes it, too." Isabelle shook her head. "Well, the school can kiss my booty. The important question is what are *we* going to be all about this year?"

"What were we all about last year?" Erik asked.

"Nothing—that's why we need to figure out what our mission will be now. Come on guys, we don't want to waste another year doing nothing."

"It's not a bad idea," Maxine chimed in. "We should try to do *something* different."

"I'm not sure what I'm getting myself into, but I'm game, I guess," Erik agreed.

"Let's make a pact!" Isabelle thrust her hand into the space between them. The other two stacked their hands on top of hers.

"One week from today we'll each bring in an idea that will impact our Sophomore Year in some fabulous way," she proclaimed.

"Ready, set, go! Shazaam!" The trio threw their hands into the air.

Chapter Two

Isabelle unfolded her crumpled schedule and bee-lined toward the theater building. "Sorry, Mrs. B.," she called in the direction of her former art teacher's room. "Another muse is calling."

Mr. Kinney's drama classes were an institution at Foresthill High. He had a reputation for bucking the system and delighting it at the same time. While the rumors about this eccentric teacher repelled many students, Isabelle was drawn like a magnet.

Even after his students were seated, Mr. Kinney remained in the back of the room. A few people twisted around to see what he was doing. When Mr. Kinney didn't budge, murmurs arose that maybe their teacher was crazy. Isabelle smiled and said, "I like crazy" under her breath.

When he finally decided to move, Mr. Kinney took his time strolling to the front of the classroom. Isabelle's eyes followed him. She decided that he looked like a thin Santa Claus, with his white hair and beard and ruddy cheeks. His twinkling blue eyes fulfilled the Irish stereotype and a slight limp in his left leg marred his otherwise fit body.

Facing the class, Mr. Kinney asked, "Does anyone fancy why I was standing in the back when you came in?"

"*Fancy?*" someone chuckled.

No one offered a theory, including Isabelle, who had a dozen swirling around in her mind.

He answered for himself. "I'm not going to be in the front of the classroom, lecturing or telling you exactly what to do. I will, however, be behind you, coaching you, prodding you, and tapping into your creativity. You'll only learn what you put into it."

"What's he on?" a boy near Isabelle whispered.

"The 60's, I think," another boy answered. He bobbled his head and bulged out his eyes.

"Let's get started then, shall we?" Mr. Kinney proposed. "Everyone get into a circle."

"I'm dropping this crazy-ass class," the first boy grumbled as he stood up.

"If he makes us hold hands, I'm outta here," the second one agreed.

Isabelle positioned herself across the room near her teacher. By the end of the drama warm-ups, nobody had bailed. Instead, their swelling laughter spilled past the door and into the hallway. She couldn't believe it when the bell rang so soon after they started.

Isabelle lingered, pretending to arrange her books in her backpack. On her way out, she paused at Mr. Kinney's desk. "I'm going to like this class," she stated.

"I hope you do."

"That activity was cool." Isabelle scuffed her shoe against the edge of his desk. "Thanks for making it fun."

He nodded. "You're very welcome, Ms. Foxfire." She blushed at the roll of his tongue on her name.

Isabelle broke into a gallop. When she located her target standing in the middle of the courtyard, she tackled him from behind.

"God, Isabelle! You nearly gave me a heart attack!" Erik clutched his chest. "You can't just run up on a person like that!"

"Stop acting like you're eighty!" She kissed him on the ear. "Or I'm gonna get you a walker."

"What are you so hyper about?"

"Erik, my drama teacher is so awesome. He's like this weird, old Irish beatnik. I can't wait to start acting."

"*Start* acting? When have you ever stopped?"

"What are you implying?"

"The words 'drama queen' come to mind." Erik smiled as he delivered the verdict.

"Yeah? Well, so what? At least I'll get a good grade for doing what I do naturally."

"I think it'll be a great year for you, Bella. Maybe even *perfect*. Speaking of which, what's really going on with you and Maxine?"

Isabelle hopped off the sidewalk and began walking with one foot in the gutter and the other on the curb. "Mr. Kinney is so hot! He reminds me of Sean Connery."

"Earth to Isabelle." Erik waved his hand in front of her gaze. "Don't ignore my question."

"Huh?" She looked up just in time to avoid crashing into a stop sign. "What are you talking about?"

"It's a little disturbing to hear you call your drama teacher 'hot'." Erik steered her towards home.

"He is, though. I think I'll have a crush on him this year. Nothing major, just for fun." She drew a heart in the air with her finger and sky-wrote, "Isabelle + Mr. Kinney."

Erik shuddered. "It's just not right."

"Well, you better get used to it." Isabelle motioned to the invisible heart and snickered.

"I'd much rather talk about your other crush. Spill it, girlfriend." Erik didn't mince words, lest Isabelle get distracted again.

Isabelle fell into step beside him. "Maxine is my best friend, besides you, of course," she answered. "There's nothing going on."

"How long do you think it's going to stay that way?"

"Hey, I'm pretty happy not being in love," Isabelle replied. "After Mandy, I don't think I really want to go there again anytime soon."

"Have you seen her yet?"

"I caught a glance of her at lunch but she was pretty well blockaded by jockstraps—probably to protect her from the ravaging lesbian who seduced her last year."

"It turns out she's in my yearbook class. It's weird—she seems like a stranger."

"Really? I wonder if she dropped out of honors English because of me."

"Yeah, I noticed she wasn't there, too. How are you feeling about that whole situation?"

"Stupid more than anything. I still don't understand how she could totally change right in front of my eyes. Was I just a little diversion for her?" Isabelle pondered. "Whatever—it's a big school. Our paths don't have to cross without us wanting them to."

"True enough."

"People are still talking trash about me, though. I may have to set them straight!" Isabelle smacked her palms like cymbals. "Pardon the pun."

"I'm glad I'm not them. I'd hate to be on the receiving end of Isabelle Foxfire."

"Don't tell anyone," Isabelle whispered. "But a dose of ridicule is much sweeter than revenge."

Erik put his hand on the back of Isabelle's neck. "Well, I'm just happy you're doing better. Last year had me a little bit worried."

Lingering in front of Isabelle's front walk, Erik dug a little deeper. "But you do know that Maxine has the hots for you, right?"

"She tell you that?"

"No, but it's really obvious. Bella, pay attention. Just see how she looks at you, how close she tries to be."

"Erik, stop stirring things up. We're just friends. And, if she really liked me that way, don't you think I would know by now?"

"No offense, Isabelle, but you're pretty oblivious to what's happening outside of your own little world. Remember what she wrote in your yearbook?"

"Well, it's not going to happen right now. Maybe never. Even with my mad skills, I can't predict the future."

"Don't shut out the possibility of falling in love again," he advised.

"What's wrong with preferring to be alone? I don't need to be in love with someone else to be whole, you know?" She repeated her therapist's mantra.

Erik yielded his argument for the moment. "Final thought: I just want to see you happy and I think Maxine would be good for you."

"Thanks, Dr. Phil. But I'm going to stick with Mr. Kinney. Now get home and call your own honey."

"Okay, sis. Talk to you later."

Isabelle stood outside of her house a few minutes longer, thinking about Erik's words. Throughout the summer, Isabelle would periodically pull out her yearbook and smooth her fingers over the indentations that Maxine's pen had left in the corner of the glossy page. The message often flickered around the edges of Isabelle's consciousness. Even though Maxine had stirred up new feelings in Isabelle, which gradually shoved Mandy to the perimeter of her heart, Isabelle didn't want to ruin the first blossoming friendship she'd had with another girl since elementary school. So, fighting her hormones and winning for the time being, Isabelle remained in the celibate state she'd declared after the breakup.

Chapter Three

Isabelle twisted the door handle and tossed her sweater onto a hook by the door. "La, la, la, la in the neighborhood, tra la la la...I'm ho-ome!" She bellowed through the house and then stopped in front of the hall mirror to pick at a scab on her newest piercing.

"I want to hear about your first day of school." Ana's voice resonated back.

"In a minute, Mom." Isabelle went into the kitchen and grabbed a banana before seeking out her mother's location. "Hey, there you are," she said, when she found her mother amidst a pile of junk in the garage. "What are you doing?"

"Looking for something," Ana answered, digging through a soggy cardboard box.

"Uh, that's obvious. Can I help?" Isabelle played with the gummi bracelets on her wrist.

Ana's tousled head looked up. "Grab a box," she said, indicating which one with her chin.

Isabelle sat down on the oil-stained cement next to her mother. "Are you going to tell me what exactly we're looking for?"

Her mother's hands ceased rifling through yellowing papers and she answered, "I'm looking for this essay I wrote in grad school. I'm working on an article for *Mother Jones* magazine this month."

"Do you know what it's titled?" Isabelle asked, as she opened the crusty box in front of her and started sifting through papers.

"I don't really remember, but you'll probably see 'Vietnam' at the top," Ana said. "So, how did it go today?"

"School was pretty typical. I don't feel any different from being a freshman, except that I know where everything is this year. I do have one class that's going to be interesting. The jury is still out on the others."

"English?" Ana guessed.

"English will be okay. But I have Mr. Paulson this year and I'm not sure he has a sense of humor."

"I can't imagine what else it might be—certainly not math!" Ana looked up from her box. "I give up."

"It's drama. Mr. Kinney rocks. He said that we even get to put on a play. Maybe I'll get the guts to try out."

"You should. Acting is right up your alley, Izzy."

"Well, I'm already an art nerd, so I guess adding drama geek to my resume won't ruin my reputation any further," Isabelle stated.

"Just remember—nerds end up running the world," her mother answered.

They dug through the boxes for the next few minutes, extracting mildewed papers and curled photographs. "Is this you?" Isabelle handed Ana a wallet-sized picture of a young girl in a long brown coat lined with fake sheepskin.

The girl wore auburn hair and oversized sunglasses, smiling for the camera.

"God, I haven't seen this in ages! Yep, that's me, all right." She squinted at the image.

"How old are you there?"

"A little older than you are. Let's see," she said, turning the picture over to read the faded date on the back. "1969: I was a freshman in college. Wow—this brings me back."

"Tell me," Isabelle begged.

"Another time, Isabelle," Ana answered. "Let's not talk about the past. What about the future? What would you like to see happen in your lifetime?"

"Funny you should ask. We were just having that conversation at lunch. But I don't know what to do. None of us do. My generation has nothing to care about."

"Oh Isabelle, there are plenty of things to care about. Be happy that you don't have to face what my generation did. Besides, there are plenty of injustices still going on here in good ol' America," Ana replied.

"But what can we do? Nobody really gives a crap what teenagers have to say."

"Don't lose faith. You may have more impact than you think. Just do what you want to do, regardless of whether it ends up changing anything or not. The journey is what's important, not necessarily the result."

"You sound like a fortune cookie, Mom."

Ana laughed. "I'm just trying to inspire you."

Isabelle went back to her box. "Yeah, you know I always come up with something."

"Without a doubt," Ana replied.

"I don't think that paper you're looking for is in here," Isabelle said, after pulling out the last object from the tattered carton.

"Thanks for helping me look," Ana said. "It was nice to catch up with you."

"No problem." Isabelle untwisted her legs and stood up. "I guess I'll get dinner started."

Studying the chores schedule on the fridge, Isabelle teetered on the toes of her Converse All-Stars like a misbegotten ballerina. As she delved into the contents of the cupboards, Isabelle mulled over the pact she'd initiated at lunchtime. "I've got a whole week to figure something out. Plenty of time," she told herself. "Now if I could just figure out what to make for dinner..."

Much to Isabelle's surprise, the first week marched by as though school had never let out for the summer. Students slid back into their cliques, habits, and attitudes like salmon returning to their spawning site. Kids who'd vowed to turn over a new leaf and make better grades, hang out with different people, and not get into trouble, were already lining the Principal's office walls and arguing with teachers about missing assignments.

Determined not to let this year mirror last year, Isabelle reminded her friends that D-Day was coming. "Bring in some good ideas or else," she forewarned.

Unconcerned with Isabelle's threats, Erik spent the evening on the phone with Jeremy just like he'd grown accustomed to over the summer. While at work, Erik's father hadn't been able to monitor his son's correspondences and, even if they weren't able to see each other in person, the couple found ways to talk every day. Physical distance created urgency between them. Heated conversations fueled their fires, sparked by that first kiss in the darkened hallway at Lakepark High last spring.

At first they were only able to meet in public places, electricity coursing between them even when they weren't touching. The saving grace came when Jeremy announced, mid-summer, that his best friend had passed his driver's test. A car not only meant freedom from parental drop-offs and pick-ups, but privacy as well. Adam, who was straight but not narrow, allowed Erik and Jeremy time alone in his SUV while he shopped for girls at the mall or hung out at the arcade. His Ford Bronco had tinted windows and provided a safe haven.

By summer's end, Erik found himself so wrapped up in love that he thought about little else other than Jeremy. He wanted to avoid getting himself into the same situation Isabelle had fallen into with Mandy, but found it more difficult than he anticipated. Every conversation deepened their relationship, but the distance across town limits added strain.

Pushing his homework aside, Erik huddled under his covers and dialed Jeremy's number. "Hey sexy," he whispered. "How was your first week of school?"

"Better if you were with me. But not bad overall."

"Anything interesting to report?"

"Not so far. You know we live in the most boring towns in the universe," Jeremy replied.

"Isabelle is trying to liven things up by making us come up with some cause to take on. I'm supposed to bring in an idea tomorrow," Erik said.

"Leave it to Isabelle. What are you thinking of?"

"You want to be part of it?"

"Depends on what it is."

"You'll be the first to know when I come up with something," Erik answered.

"How about a 'Save the Albino Gorillas' crusade?" Jeremy suggested.

"Oh, I can see you're going to be a real help!" Erik poked his head above the covers to take a breath of fresh air. "I need something realistic."

"Seriously, what are you interested in?"

"You should know that by now—cute boys with dimples and freckles."

"We're getting somewhere now." Jeremy flirted back. "I have just the cause for you—come on over and I'll show you. It's *very* realistic."

"I wish," Erik said. "But for now, I should come up with something for real or Isabelle'll throttle me."

"You need some problem to be solved, right? What about something like a river clean-up campaign? That place gets thrashed once summer's over."

"Hey, that's a pretty good idea, nature boy."

"I'll take that as a compliment," Jeremy said.

"Everything I say to you is a compliment. You're the best thing that's ever happened to me."

"Aw shucks."

"Time's a tickin'—I better hang up now," Erik said. "We'll talk tomorrow, okay?"

"Come on, just a leetle bit longer?" Jeremy whined.

"You know the game plan. We don't want my dad—or yours for that matter—to catch on," Erik reminded him for the hundredth time.

"Yeah, yeah, yeah. Get back in that closet, boy." Jeremy made a whipping sound.

"Thanks for the river clean-up idea. I'll probably pitch it, even though I can't picture Isabelle spending a day picking up garbage."

"Just tell her that we'll bring her some cheerleaders in short skirts to help out."

"You want me to get killed? I'm pretty sure Isabelle's done with cheerleaders," Erik alleged.

"Never say never."

"Crap—I think I hear footsteps."

"Good night, my sweet," Jeremy answered. He rolled over and pulled a spiral-bound journal out of his backpack. On the first blank page he wrote, "Today was a good day...not at all like yesterday."

Across town, Erik opened his lit book and glanced over the short story Mr. Paulson assigned for homework. It was about a man who was like a chameleon; every time he entered a different situation he turned into whatever that situation required—a different race, gender, social class, and so on. At the end of the story, he walked into an empty room with blank walls and disappeared forever.

Erik reread the prompt for a third time: *How does the theme of this story reflect your own life?* He pressed his pen against his notebook and wrote, "I'm afraid I might become this man." Erik chewed the tip of his pen, wondering what to write next.

His father interrupted with a knock at the door. Jack stuck his face in the crack. "Almost finished with your homework," he asked.

"I've got a little more to write for English and then I'll get to bed."

"On your way to getting straight A's again this year?"

"Without a question. My classes are pretty easy. Nothing to worry about." Erik wished his father would just shut the door, but he opened it wider and looked around the room.

"Uh, anything else?" Erik asked, shielding the first sentence of his composition with his elbow.

Jack finished his surveillance and backed out of the room. "No son. Good night."

When the door was securely shut, Erik lifted his arm off the paper and saw that he'd smeared the ink. It looked like he'd written, "I'mafraidImightbecomethisman."

Erik crumbled up the paper and set a clean sheet on the desk. He wrote, "The theme of this story is that people who seem to profit from changing their identities just to fit in, actually end up sacrificing the most important thing— their individuality. Just look at Foresthill High for evidence of this theme over and over again..."

Chapter Four

"Nothing more ridiculous than a pep rally," Isabelle complained to Mr. Kinney as their class filed out of the theater room. "Can't I just stay inside and practice my scene? Nobody has to know." She crossed her heart.

"Think of it as a character study," her drama teacher coached. "Instead of being annoyed, be amused."

"That does make it sound more appealing," she agreed. "As long as I don't have to be peppy."

"You may surprise yourself."

"I doubt it." Isabelle took a deep breath and entered the flow.

As the masses filled the gym in waves, Isabelle sought out Maxine. Gazing too far into the sea of bodies, she collided into the person in front of her. The throng behind her had swept her into a momentum in which she could only move forward. When the girl turned around, Isabelle stopped cold, the word "sorry" having already left her lips.

Mandy's face flashed with color when she realized it was Isabelle crushing up against her backpack. Isabelle looked away and willed Mandy to turn around and disappear. Instead, Mandy angled next to her.

"How are you?" Mandy asked. "I've been meaning to talk to you for awhile now."

"I'm okay." Isabelle tried to increase the space between them, but people kept pushing her into Mandy's ribcage.

"Well, I'm still feeling bad about what happened."

"Sorry to hear that," Isabelle mumbled, as she scanned the crowd. Her eyes darted anywhere other than the person next to her.

"Listen, I want to explain..." Mandy tried to reboot herself onto Isabelle's radar.

Spotting Maxine a few yards away, Isabelle cut her off. "Don't worry about explaining anything. Everything's cool. No worries."

"Wait, Isabelle. There's something I need you to understand," Mandy said to Isabelle's departing figure.

Maxine, who had been watching the whole encounter, suppressed the jealousy that rose into her throat with a bitter tang. "Don't be stupid," she told herself. "It's not a big deal."

As Isabelle joined her, Maxine searched her face, looking for any remnants of love that being near Mandy might have stoked. When Isabelle grabbed her hand and led her to the top of the bleachers, Maxine's fears dissolved and all she could think about was never wanting that hand to let her go.

Principal Martinez stood in the middle of the basketball court with a microphone in hand. Tapping the head of it with his forefinger produced such a screech of feedback that everyone clapped their hands over their ears. "Well, I guess that's one way to get you quiet."

"Welcome back to Foresthill High. Today is our first pep rally of the year. Let's welcome this year's student body president, Carmen Melerno!"

As Carmen bounced onto the stage, Isabelle turned to Maxine. "Distract me," she demanded. "Or I'm going to lose my mind."

Maxine giggled. "Let's play 'Would You Rather?'"

In a high-pitched voice, Carmen began her speech. "Hey Wildcats—wuz up! Are we going to have the best year ever or what? Wooo-Hooo!"

"Woo-Hoo?" Isabelle mouthed. "I've got one. Would you rather be locked in a room with Carmen and have to listen to this speech for 24 hours straight or have someone razor blade your fingertips?"

"Dang. That's harsh. How many of my fingertips?"

"Every single one."

"I'd have to choose Carmen." Maxine grimaced. "Psychological pain is better than physical."

"Oh I beg to differ. Now you," Isabelle instructed.

"Let me think."

As Maxine conjured up a dastardly combination, Isabelle watched the cheerleaders run out into the middle of the gym and begin their routine. She couldn't help but single Mandy out and hope that she might trip and bring the others down with her.

"I'm ready." Maxine interrupted Isabelle's fantasy. "Would you rather have to do a pole dance in a bikini in front of the whole school or join the cheerleading team for an entire year?"

"That's low, Maxine. Really low." Isabelle rubbed her hands on her jeans. She squeezed her eyes tight and squeaked, "Pole dance."

"Geez, you must really despise cheerleading."

"Not cheerleading itself," Isabelle corrected. "Just certain cheerleaders."

The pep squad ran offstage and was replaced by a parade of fall athletes in uniform. "Will the torture ever end?" Isabelle moaned. Then she remembered Mr. Kinney's suggestion. "Do you know any of these people?"

Maxine shook her head and said, "Not a one. You know I'm a hermit."

"Maybe we should actually join a club or something this year."

"Are you serious?" Maxine shouted over the marching band reverberating off the gym walls.

"I might be. It could be good for us to branch out and make some more friends."

Maxine lifted the back of her hand to Isabelle's forehead. "Are you feeling okay?"

"Just trying to amuse myself."

The principal returned to the stage and said, "Thanks for all of the hard work you students put into this assembly. You are what make Foresthill High the best school around!"

"Yee Haw!" Isabelle shouted from the stands.

Maxine ducked as those around them shot the girl in purple pigtails dirty looks. "You may want to reconsider your methods of branching out and making new friends."

Erik, who was seated with the fall athletes, waited until the flow dwindled to a trickle out the double doors. As he exited, he heard a voice call out, "Erik?" and then the squeak of tennis shoes scuffing across the floor. It took him only a moment to recognize the owner of the voice.

"Mark, right?" Erik said. "How's it going?"

"Yeah, we had history together last year, remember?"

Erik did remember, but he also remembered that Mark was also associated with Jacob Schmidt, the bully that tried to make his life a living hell his freshman year. Even though Mark had apologized for his part in the harassment, Erik was still wary of him. "Good to see you," Erik said and turned to leave.

"School's out. Where are you going?" Mark fell into step beside Erik.

"I forgot my math book in my Trig teacher's room," Erik replied. "Then I have cross-country practice."

"Trig? You're only a sophomore. How is that possible?" Mark asked.

Erik shrugged. "I took geometry last year."

"Man, I can't even pass algebra. I'm taking it *again* this semester. Maybe I should get a tutor," he hinted.

"Well, this is the room. See you later, Mark." Erik stopped short and opened the door.

"Catch ya later—I'm off to football practice," Mark said, tossing his shaggy hair out of his eyes. With a puzzled look on his face, Erik watched Mark lope back down the hallway toward the gym.

Chapter Five

"Well, today's the day," Isabelle said, as she unwrapped her tofu pita and took a bite. "What have you got kids?"

"I was thinking about what you said at the pep rally," Maxine said. "Maybe we could start a club."

"What kind of club?" Isabelle probed.

"Something artsy. I thought we might be allowed to paint a mural on the side of the school."

"Hey, that sounds pretty cool," Isabelle said.

"Ahem," Erik interrupted. "Doesn't that leave out some people with no artistic talent?"

Maxine replied, "I thought of that. But I couldn't come up with anything else appealing. Sorry buddy."

"How about a play?" Isabelle offered. "Then everyone could be involved. Erik, you could write or do behind the scenes work, Max could paint sets, and I could star in it."

They laughed at her last comment. "Of course, you'd have to be the star," Maxine agreed.

Isabelle gesticulated wildly. "I didn't mean it to come out that way. It was just an idea."

"Does anyone want to hear my proposal?" Erik asked.

"Yes, yes, yes. We're not leaving you out." Isabelle turned toward Erik and folded her hands in her lap.

"I was thinking we could put together like a 10k run for charity and then donate the money.

"What kind of charity?"

"Anything we want. Cancer Society, SPCA, Save the Albino Gorillas—whatever appeals to us."

"Well, it's obvious where all of our talents lie," Maxine observed. "Actually, I think Erik's idea would work best, though. People love to pull together and run their guts out for some odd reason."

Isabelle smiled. "You've got a point there. Erik, what do you think it would take to organize it?"

"No clue. Let me talk to my cross country coach and see what he thinks."

"Great! Let's decide on a charity," Maxine said.

"You want to do some research after school today?" Isabelle touched Maxine's hand.

"Meet me in the library," Maxine answered.

Isabelle ran to her drama class, the wheels in her mind spinning so fast that her body couldn't keep up. As she swung the door open, she nearly knocked Mr. Kinney over. "Oh my God, I'm sorry, Mr. Kinney! I need to slow down."

"Couldn't wait to get here, huh, Isabelle?" he said.

"More true than you know." She grinned and lowered her eyelashes at him.

"Take a seat, Isabelle." Mr. Kinney turned toward the class. "All right, everyone, get out a piece of paper."

Isabelle sat down and obeyed. She began making a list of all the things that she could think of to bring their vision into reality. Meanwhile, Mr. Kinney went over to his CD player and pressed play. The first chords of an Irish folk tune sprinkled out of the speakers and soon consumed the airspace in the room. "Now write," he instructed.

"Anything you want to write. But don't pick up your pen until I say so."

The room was silent except for students breathing and pencils scratching on paper. Isabelle wrote, sometimes in prose, sometimes in limerick, on the lines and outside of the lines, with delicacy and ferocity. She wrote and wrote, page after page, ignoring the cramping in her hand and the droplet of blood emerging from her cuticle.

When Mr. Kinney flicked the lights off and on again, Isabelle laid her pen to rest and unclenched her writing fist. It was only then that she tended to the blood creeping from her wound. Isabelle pressed her finger onto the corner of her paper and made a scarlet print.

While waiting for her teacher's next instruction, Isabelle doodled around the blood stain and turned it into a rose. Then she reread her scribblings.

What are these masks we wear?
Alone and hiding scared.
To pull them off,
One might scoff
To find there's nothing there.

When the wind stirs up the dust,
We cover our eyes in the gust.
Shrinking from gales,
Like runaway snails
With only our shells to trust.

Love cannot be unraveled
Like the hem of a dress well-traveled
Tossed in the trash,
A secret stash
In silent words we babble.

Love remains,
When all else is gone.
Everything made can be unmade.

"For homework," Mr. Kinney began. "I want you to take one idea, one line, or one emotion from what you just wrote and create a short dramatic scene around it. One or two pages should suffice. Just take a stab at it and we'll see what you come up with tomorrow."

"I've got just the idea, Mr. Kinney!" Isabelle bounced outside to embrace the warmth of the afternoon sun and a waiting Maxine in the library.

Isabelle leaned against the heavy door and saw the back of Maxine's head at a computer station. She crept up behind her and set her hands on Maxine's shoulders. Maxine leaned her head back and smiled upside down at Isabelle. "Take a seat," she said. "I just got online."

Isabelle rolled a chair close to Maxine's and flopped down. Her knee bumped Maxine's as she scooted closer. "Oops. Sorry."

Maxine raised an eyebrow. "I'm not."

"Then I take it back." Isabelle grinned.

Balancing a pad of paper on Isabelle's lap, Maxine said, "Okay, we need to gather the who, what, where, when, why, and how."

"Gotcha," Isabelle said, as they embarked on a series of searches to fuel their venture.

Until the librarian called out, "Five minutes to closing," the girls brainstormed ideas and attempted to create a plan for the event.

"At this point, I think we need Erik's input," Isabelle said, and shoved a pencil behind her ear.

"Good work today." Maxine gestured to the notebook. She held out her hand and Isabelle gave it to her, making sure that their fingers brushed during the transaction.

"Are you walking home?" Maxine asked, as they exited the campus.

"As usual."

"My mom could probably drive you."

"I'll take a rain check on that. I could use some fresh air," Isabelle replied.

"Okay." Maxine tried to hide the disappointment on her face. "Call me tonight?"

"I have this scene to write for Mr. Kinney."

"See you tomorrow then." Maxine stepped into the gutter and faced the oncoming traffic.

Isabelle stood on the sidewalk trying to find something to say. "Okay bye," was all she could come up with. As she headed home, she asked herself, "What's my problem? Maxine deserves better."

Half a block from her house, Isabelle sat down on the curb and opened her notebook. "Choose an emotion, an idea, or a line and create a scene," she read aloud. Flipping to a blank sheet of paper, Isabelle wrote at the top:

"An Existential Love Story"
Scene 1: Two people across the Grand Canyon from each other.

Person 1: Can you hear me? [echoing across the canyon]
Person 2: Can I hear you? [echoing back]
Person 1: Can you see me?
Person 2: Can I see you?
Person 1: Come over here.
Person 2: You come over here.
Person 1: The view is better from where I stand.

Person 2: No, the view is better from where I stand.
Person 1: If you come here, you'll be happier.
Person 2: If you come here, you'll be safer.
Person 1: But I don't see how...
Person 2: ...to get over there.
Person 1: Climb.
Person 2: Fly.
Person 1: Jump.
Person 2: Swing.
Person 1: But what if I die?
Person 2: Love is stronger than death.
Person 1: Not if I die.
Person 2: Can't you just try?
Person 1: And if I do?
Person 2: You'll see.
Person 1: And if I don't?
Person 2: You'll never know.
Person 1: Know what?
Person 2: What its worth.
Person 1: What's 'it'?
Person 2: Love.
Person 1: What? I can't hear you.
Person 2: You can't hear me?
Person 1: Where? I can't see you.
Person 2: You can't see me?
Person 1: Come over here.
Person 2: You come over here.

Chapter Six

They never talked about it openly. The subverted feelings. The acknowledgment of mutual attraction. The connection they both felt that went beyond friendship. No. They mostly talked about their dreams and plans, and the meaning of life, but nothing so intimate that their true feelings might surface. Many days they lay side-by-side on a grassy knoll in the nether regions of Maxine's estate, inches away from each other, but never touching.

Maxine lived on a ranch with her parents and a bevy of other animals. Isabelle called it "The Ark". One early morning, on the last day of summer, the girls worked together to feed the pigs their slop and toss hay into the stalls for the livestock. As they entered the barn, Isabelle said, "I love the way it smells in here. It's so cozy."

"I thought I was the only one turned on by the smell of manure," Maxine had replied. The horses nickered and whinnied when they heard the girls coming armed with sugar cubes.

"I could stay here forever," Isabelle announced, settling down on a bale of hay. Maxine smiled, but didn't say what she was thinking. She merely looked at Isabelle, wondering how to make that wish come true.

This evening, however, as Maxine did her chores alone, her memories of that last night of summer seemed dim. Stabbing the pitchfork into a loose bale of hay and flinging it into the stable, Maxine's muscles strained with satisfaction. Though small, Maxine was strong. She could lift her own body weight in hay and wrestle a runaway goat into submission. She didn't look like a typical farm girl, however, with her petite frame and foreign features. Maxine's paternal grandfather had emigrated from Japan and married a half-Apache and half-Caucasian woman whom he'd met while traveling cross country. They settled in Foresthill and established the Kotamo ranch where Maxine's family still lived.

Maxine's quiet intellect, coupled with her mysterious demeanor, kept most people at bay. She was too beautiful to be approached, though most high school boys wouldn't put her on their "top ten list" of most attractive girls. Maxine, however, was only concerned about being number one on Isabelle's list.

Being multiracial, Maxine was forever being asked, "What *are* you, anyway?" To which she had ceased coming up with witty answers.

Isabelle couldn't believe that Maxine refused to defend herself whenever people made racial comments. Just yesterday, she had witnessed Isabelle verbally take on a group of kids after school, while she remained silent.

"Goddamn towel-heads!" one of them had exclaimed. "America should just send those Arabians back where they came from!"

"But then we'd have no 7-11's, man," someone said.

Another responded, "That's fine with me. We need to take back America anyway!"

"Well, we're gonna bomb the hell out of those camel jockeys soon, though. I heard something about the military being sent over to Afgaziland."

"You mean Af*ghanistan*?" The whole group stopped talking and turned to face Isabelle.

Maxine saw the speaker give her a look as if to say, "Who the hell are you?"

"I just have one question." Isabelle tapped her chin in mock contemplation.

"Yeah, what do you want to know? Which one of us is going to turn you straight?" a boy asked.

"Oh honey, that's so sad," Isabelle replied.

"What the hell do you want anyway?" the apparent ringleader asked.

"I just wanted to ask if any of you is Native American."

"Native American? You mean, like an Indian?" The boys looked at each other and shook their heads.

"All of your families immigrated here at some point in history, right?" Isabelle continued, while Maxine watched from a few yards away.

Again, they nodded in unison. "What's your point?"

"Well, I just thought that I should bring it to your attention that, unless we are Native Americans, we are all immigrants from somewhere. So when you suggest sending people back to their 'own' countries, I would encourage you to do a little research about where you're going to be sent."

"Oh, aren't you smart?"

"Actually, I am. That's why I don't make ignorant comments that give Americans a bad name." Isabelle then turned on her heel and called over her shoulder. "You have a brain, why don't you use it?"

When she rejoined Maxine, Isabelle was grinning from ear to ear. "Ah, I love doing a little social justice."

31

Consumed with her thoughts about Isabelle, Maxine stayed out in the barn with her horses until the sun slipped over the horizon. She sang and nuzzled them until it was too dark to see. Lighting the gas lantern, hanging by the barn door, Maxine illuminated her path back to the house. It was a journey that Isabelle liked to call the *Little House on the Prairie* walk. Maxine giggled as she remembered Isabelle tripping on the way back to the house in the dark, pretending to be Laura Ingalls Wilder.

As she walked alone tonight, Maxine paid close attention to what some would call silence around her. Crickets chirped in symphony with frogs, the crackle of twigs beneath her feet, providing a fine percussion. The tinkling of the creek that ran through their property babbled the unspoken language of nature. Looking up at the thousands of stars speckling the sky, Maxine imagined she could hear their glow. She felt as though the blackness blanketing her was protecting her from any horror the night might hold. "If only the whole world could be like this," she thought.

Not wanting to go inside just yet, Maxine sat and rocked on the porch swing. Inside her head, she composed yet another letter to Isabelle that she knew would never be sent. Since last year, Maxine had ceased putting notes in Isabelle's locker and kept her attraction in check while in her presence. Though she perceived a change in her best friend's feelings towards her, she was determined to wait until Isabelle made the first move. After this afternoon's parting, however, Maxine was beginning to doubt that Isabelle would ever come around.

In her mind, she whispered the things she could never say aloud:

I wish you could share this night with me. No one else would appreciate it as much as you. It's starting to rain and I'm sitting here under the protection of the porch watching puddles form in the field. I can hear the horses down in the stable whinnying at the rain. I close my eyes and imagine you sitting here next to me, holding me in your arms, and whispering into my hair. We can smell the smoke of the wood burning in the fireplace inside. We live here alone; this world is ours. I get up to wrap a blanket around us and you say, 'Hurry back.' And as I dream this, I can almost feel you here. Will it ever be, Isabelle?

Maxine closed her eyes and listened to the rain drumming on the awning. The screen door creaked and Maxine's father stepped onto the porch. "Honey?"

"Yeah Papa?"

"You have a phone call," he said, holding out the cordless phone.

"Thanks." She reached up and put the receiver to her ear. "Hello?"

"It's Iz. What are you up to?"

Maxine couldn't help but smile. "Oh, not much. Just enjoying the rain."

"It's raining?"

"Yeah silly. It's starting to pour," she said, just as the first boom of thunder rumbled in the sky.

"I guess I was caught up. I just finished my scene for Mr. Kinney's class."

"What's it about?" Maxine asked.

"Love. Sort of."

"Want to read it to me?"

"Not quite yet."

"Any idea when?"

"I wish I did."

"I'll be here when you're ready."

Isabelle pressed the phone against her ear. "How's the view over there?"

"Beautiful. Want to come over?"

"Yes. But I can't."

"I know."

"Yeah, you always seem to."

Chapter Seven

The next day at lunch, the trio met up to discuss their plans. "Here's the deal," Erik summarized. "We need to publicize the event, get sponsorship to pay for it, call the Foresthill and Lake Park town halls to get the proper permits, and then do the actual set up for the race."

"Sounds like a huge amount of work. How much time do we have?" Isabelle asked.

"Just about three weeks," Maxine answered. "We're going to need more bodies."

"Maybe we should put it in the bulletin and see if anyone shows up to a meeting," Isabelle suggested.

"My coach said that he'd get the team involved. That's about twenty people right there," Erik said.

"Perfect. Will you organize on that end? Isabelle and I can mock up some posters and write up announcements." Maxine glanced at Isabelle for confirmation.

"If we take one major action a day, I think we can make this happen," Isabelle stated.

From a nearby table, Mandy had been keeping one eye on Isabelle until the bell dismissed them to their classes.

Just from the few weeks she and Isabelle had been intimate last spring, Mandy felt like she was able to interpret Isabelle's moods, even from afar. "She must be planning something," Mandy concluded.

Extracting herself from her friends, Mandy followed a few dozen yards behind Isabelle as she skipped off to class. Though she had convinced herself that their relationship could never work, Mandy was still intrigued and captivated by this intangible quality of her former love.

Arriving late to yearbook class, Mandy plunked her books down on the table, and rested her chin on her hands while her teacher took attendance. It was an action that did not go unnoticed by Erik, who was already sifting through pictures when Mandy walked in. He found himself pulling out a chair next to her. "Hi, how you doing?"

Mandy cocked her head and looked at him. "Hi, Erik," she said. "Okay, considering..." She squeezed her eyes shut.

"Listen, if you want to take a walk, I'm sure Mrs. Wang won't mind," Erik offered.

"I'm all right, Erik. It's nice of you to ask."

Erik scraped his chair back and prepared to stand up.

"Does she ever talk about me?" Mandy mumbled into her hands.

"Excuse me?" He leaned forward.

"Isabelle. I miss her." Mandy's voice wavered. "It's not the same without her."

Erik lowered his voice in response. "Isabelle's doing better now. She's a lot healthier than before."

Mandy looked to him to answer her original question.

"Um, no. She doesn't really mention you anymore. I think she's put that in the past," Erik disclosed.

"Who's that girl I always see her with?" Mandy's eyes searched Erik's face.

"You know, I'm not really sure that Isabelle would want me talking to you about her personal life, so I'm going to shut up now." Erik tried to make it sound like a joke.

"I guess she'll never want to be my friend again, huh?"

"That's up to Isabelle but, if you want my advice, give her some more time. I'm sorry you're still hurting."

"Not every day," Mandy said. "Just when no one seems to understand."

Erik patted her on the back and then went back to work on his layout. Mandy didn't budge for the rest of the class period, even when approached by her classmates and teacher. "I don't want to talk about it," she lied over and over. The truth was, however, she did want to talk but really had no one to talk to. No one would want to hear the truth, she decided.

Once Isabelle had shut her out completely, Mandy had resumed her past social status and was re-indoctrinated into the popular ranks. Most people forgave her trespasses and, as long as she appeared normal again, Mandy faced little opposition. The more she attempted to fit back in with her friends, however, a serious storm brewed within.

Mandy took to living two conflicting lives. On the surface, she played the role of the boy-crazy teenager, partying with the best of them. On the inside, however, Mandy's true self was shrinking and dying. She ceased caring about the things that marked her as different. No longer did she argue against her parents' unethical politics; no longer did she contest her friends' callousness to those not in their clique; no longer did any of the principles Mandy stood so passionately for survive; and no longer did any part of Mandy that Isabelle fell in love with survive.

Soon it got to be easier to swallow the bile of her ideals and values along with her beliefs. "What choice do I have?" she whispered. No matter how many options she came up with to answer that question, "Choose Isabelle" always surfaced as one of them.

Across campus in Mr. Kinney's class, Isabelle doodled on her notepad, alternately thinking about how they were going to put together the 10k run and her cryptic conversation with Maxine the night before.

Mr. Kinney broke her reverie by saying, "Today we're going to have a guest speaker. She's a professional actress who's performed all over the world. I thought she might be able to give us some insight into what it's like to be a performer. And, incidentally, she's a former student of mine from back in the day." Just as he was finishing her introduction, the guest speaker slipped through the door and shut it behind her.

"Am I late?" she asked, tiptoeing toward his desk like a guilty student. A sly grin betrayed the insincerity of her question and won Isabelle over. As she studied this new character on her stage, Isabelle realized that she had never seen hair that was truly naturally red before. This hair, falling like a curtain around the woman's translucent skin, mesmerized Isabelle until she caught the woman's eye.

No matter the embarrassment she felt at being caught staring, Isabelle couldn't look away from those mosaic eyes. It looked like someone had smashed an amber glass into a thousand pieces and then sprinkled them into her eyes. The guest speaker paused in the middle of the sentence that Isabelle wasn't listening to anyway, before breaking the gaze. Isabelle dropped her head, fighting the blush creeping into her cheeks. "God, I'm an idiot!" she thought. "Who else would get caught checking out a guest speaker?"

Isabelle buried her head in her arms. Now able to pay better attention, she caught the end of the woman's story about being on stage with Dustin Hoffman on Broadway.

"And when I went backstage on closing night, he'd filled my dressing room with bouquets of cattails." Everyone laughed except for Isabelle. "What's so funny about cattails?" she wondered.

Isabelle snuck a peek through her arms and found that if she lowered her lids halfway, she could watch and listen without distraction. The actress's name was Meg O'Malley, Isabelle learned later in the lecture. The students sat on the edges of their seats as she told tales of Hollywood parties and New York debuts. When she opened it up for questions, at least ten hands shot into the air, prompting her to woo them with stories of fame and fortune.

"How do you decide what to roles to take?" A girl in the front row asked.

Meg's laugh sprinkled through the room. "Oh, I find every role interesting. You've heard the saying, 'there are no small roles, only small actors'? But to be completely honest, I like to play women who have complicated emotions. It's such a challenge to get inside of a character who is struggling with the complexities of life." Isabelle was certain that Meg let her gaze settle on her as she spoke.

"Do you know how a movie or play is going to turn out when you're filming or rehearsing? How do you know it'll be any good?" another student asked.

"Most the time I know when I've nailed it. There are times when you just can't tell 'til you see the audience's reaction, though. That's the great part of acting—your audience gets to have the final say." Meg's face flushed as she spoke.

Isabelle raised her hand; Meg nodded at her. "How did you know you wanted to be an actress?"

She jutted her chin in Mr. Kinney's direction. "You can blame him. I'm going to warn you all—drop this class now if you don't want it to change your life."

Mr. Kinney glanced at the clock and said, "Well, well, look at that, we're almost out of time. Let's thank Meg for coming and get your homework assigned, shall we?"

The students applauded their guest speaker and booed the impending homework assignment. Mr. Kinney scrawled on the board: "Look at the scene you wrote last night and add a second scene to it."

As Meg left the room she said, "If Mr. Kinney gives you guys any trouble, just call me. I'll let you in on his secrets."

Isabelle held the door open and watched her figure stride across campus into the faculty parking lot. "Who is she and when can I see her again?" Isabelle pressed herself into the wall of the building to avoid being trampled by the horde of students vacating campus. As the crowd thinned, she stepped back inside the classroom. "Mr. Kinney?"

"Oh, you're back, Isabelle. Did you enjoy the guest speaker? Isn't she a gem?"

"Yeah, she was great. Very inspiring."

"What can I do for you?"

"Was she serious about what she said about you?"

"Isabelle, actors tend to dramatize everything they experience. I just hold up the mirror for them."

"Rock on, Mr. Kinney." Isabelle flashed him a peace sign and backed out of the room.

As soon as she arrived home, she dug out her Bert and Ernie puppets and had them enact Scene One using a laundry basket as the Grand Canyon. At the end of the dialogue, she couldn't resist dropping both puppets to their death as they reached out to meet each other.

"That's just sick," Isabelle said. "There must be another way."

Chapter Eight

Erik fumbled with his house keys to get the door open before the phone stopped ringing. Flinging his backpack against the wall, he grabbed the receiver and breathed, "Hello, Hello?"

"Erik?"

"Oh, Jeremy, I'm glad it's you," Erik said, glancing around to ensure his privacy. "Just a sec."

He didn't see anyone around, but he exited the room anyway. "Okay, I'm alone now," Erik whispered. "How did today go?"

"Who's Jeremy?"

"Who, who is this?"

"Your cousin Jamie. From San Francisco."

"Jamie! Oh my God, I haven't heard your voice in years." Erik was glad his cousin couldn't see him blushing.

"I just called to see how your family is doing. I know both Jacks are in the military. You all okay over there? Any news from the Eastern front?"

Erik gathered his thoughts. "We're all okay. My dad is 'on call' whenever there's a new terrorist threat and my brother is stationed in San Diego right now."

"How's your mom holding up?"

"She's used to it. She doesn't have much of a say anyway—you know how things are around here."

"Yeah, I remember—martial law, huh?"

"It's getting a little looser now that I'm in high school," Erik replied.

"High school, huh? How's that going? What are you—a freshman now?"

"Sophomore. It's okay. What have you been doing in San Francisco?"

"A better question is what am I *not* doing?" Jamie laughed. "Seriously, life out here is so free and there are so many opportunities."

"Like what?"

"Oh boy. I don't think I can explain that to you right now, Erik. Tell me about your life. I haven't seen you since you were a kid."

"Things haven't changed a whole lot. I'm pretty much the same person."

"Still hanging out with that crazy Isabelle chick?"

"Oh yeah, we'll be best friends forever."

"I always liked her," Jamie said. "Too much for Foresthill I bet, though."

"You got that right. People are kinda rude to her. But Isabelle doesn't care at all—she just throws it right back in their faces and makes them look stupid."

"And what about you?" Jamie asked.

"What do you mean?" Erik twirled the phone cord.

"How do people treat you?"

"Well, most everyone is cool to me. But there are some jerks. No more than any other place, I guess."

42

"Well, take care of yourself, Erik. High school can be rough enough."

"You don't need to worry, Jamie. I'm okay."

"Okay Cuz. Well, I guess I better get off the phone since you're expecting a call."

"I am?" Erik had already forgotten about the way he'd answered the phone.

"*Jeremy*, remember?"

"Oh, that. I was just..."

"It's all right, Erik. Just messing with you," Jamie said. "I forgot how literally you take everything."

"It was good to talk to you, Jamie. Maybe we can talk again sometime."

"All right, kiddo. Give your mom a big hug for me and keep me updated on the Jacks."

The moment Erik placed the receiver back on the cradle, the phone rang again.

"Meet me at the park by the river?" Jeremy's voice sounded anxious. "I just need to feel you close."

Erik looked at the clock. "I don't know. I really should be here for my mom. My dad's leaving town again."

"What about me?"

"I guess I could run down there—it'll take me about twenty minutes, though, and I could only stay for an hour."

"An hour is better than nothing at all," Jeremy replied. "Adam already said he'd drop me off there on his way to the mall."

"Okay, I'll see you around 4:30 then." Erik ended the call and tightened up his running shoes. He bounded into the bathroom and sprayed an extra dose of deodorant under his arms to waylay the inevitable sweat from his run. Erik jogged past the living room and called, "I'm going for a run, Ma. Be back before dinner."

Erik sucked in the cooling air as the sun dipped closer to the horizon. When he reached the usual spot where they'd met all summer, Erik panted and jogged in place for a few minutes to cool his body. As he was leaning over the picnic table, stretching his muscles, he heard a voice call, "Whoo, baby!" Erik dropped his leg back to the ground and laughed. "Good thing I know your voice or you would have scared the crap out of me."

Jeremy sidled up next to him and said, "Well? Where's my hug?"

Erik slid into his arms and felt his muscles cramp up. He scanned the area over Jeremy's shoulder, determining whether they were safe. Even though he didn't see anyone, he pulled back. "Hi, it's good to see you. I feel like it's been a century."

"Being away from you is making me crazy," Jeremy said. "It's good to finally see you in person."

They sat on the benches facing the river. "The sunset's beautiful, isn't it?" Erik said, playing with Jeremy's hand. He turned and looked at Jeremy's face and said, "So are you." As soon as the words came out of his mouth, he felt stupid. "I mean..."

Jeremy put his finger on Erik's lips. "Don't ruin it. That was really sweet. Tell me more."

Erik opened his mouth and invented poem after poem, unleashing his feelings. The more he spoke, the louder his heart whispered the words, "I love you, I love you, I love you," until they finally rose up out of his mouth and he couldn't swallow them back down. After this last utterance, the boys became frozen in a moment that makes or breaks a young romance.

"Do you mean it? Or was that just some poetic riff?" Jeremy asked.

Erik hesitated and said, "It's all true. It's what I feel. I'm sorry—I just can't help it."

"Sorry? Don't be sorry. I've been feeling it ever since summer and have been too afraid of saying it. I thought I'd scare you off," Jeremy confessed. "I don't know what to do with how I feel about it. It's too overwhelming. I miss you all of the time. I just keep wondering..."

"What?" Erik asked.

"Wondering how we're going to make it through. It's so damn hard being apart."

"Well, we'll both have our licenses in a couple of months, right?"

Jeremy still looked downtrodden. "Two point nine more years of high school, though, before we are really free. And who knows then?"

"Don't get all depressed on me now. We have a lot to be grateful for, don't we?"

Jeremy forced a smile. "*You* make me happy. That's about all, though."

"Come on, Jeremy. You have great friends, parents who love you, me. What else do you need?"

Jeremy didn't reply. He thought about the conversation that had taken place at lunch a few hours earlier. He debated whether or not to share it with Erik.

Jeremy had been sitting at his usual table eating lunch with his Lakepark friends when Adam asked, "Hey, are you guys going to the football game on Friday night?"

Jeremy replied, "I hadn't really thought about it."

"I thought we all might go together," Adam said.

"Sure, can you pick us up?" the boys asked.

"No problem. I've got my Bronco."

"Will there be enough room for Erik if he wants to go?" Jeremy inquired.

"I can cram about seven people in there, if you don't mind being a little squished."

"Wait—who's Erik?" one of the gang had asked the fateful question.

Adam and Jeremy exchanged glances before Jeremy said, "A friend of mine from Foresthill."

"What are you doing hanging out with Foresthill trash?" the skinny redhead named Aaron said.

"You can't be serious," Jeremy retorted. "Who believes in that stupid rivalry stuff, anyway?"

The boys shifted uncomfortably. Jeremy continued, "He's cool guys—you'll really like him. He's the one who swept that big track meet last May."

One of the boys from the track team said, "Oh, you mean Erik Pennington?"

"Yep." Jeremy nodded and smiled.

"I heard from a FH guy who goes to my church that he's a fag," Brad said.

Jeremy's face hardened. "Don't be a dick," he said.

"I'm just saying what I heard, and I heard he's a fag," Brad repeated.

Adam broke in. "Dude, just shut up about it."

"Fine," he spat, gathering up his lunch. "You can count me out for Friday if *he's* going, though. I'm not getting hit on by some pansy in the back of your truck."

"Same goes for me. Hey, wait up, Brad," Aaron said, spilling his carton of milk on the table as he hurried to catch up.

Adam and Jeremy looked at Jose and Ben, who were still sitting on the bench taking in the whole scenario. "Are you guys going to bail out, too?" Adam asked.

"Nah, it's cool. If Jeremy can vouch for him, then that's good enough," Jose claimed.

Ben piped in, "It doesn't matter to me. That guy's a great athlete. I'd love to talk to him about training."

Adam wiped up the spilled milk with his napkin and tossed the empty box in the trash. "All right then, it's settled. It'll be the five of us with room to spare."

As the bell rang and the students scattered, Adam had taken Jeremy aside and asked, "You okay, man?"

Jeremy's face didn't betray his heart. "Those guys are dumb-asses. Who cares what they think?"

Adam nodded. "We'll have fun with the other guys. They'll be cool with Erik. I just wouldn't let on if I were you—know what I mean?"

"Sure. Hey, I'll see you after school." Jeremy didn't say what he was really thinking as he walked down the hallway to his biology class. "What would happen if they knew about me?" was the recurring message flashing across the marquis in his mind. He felt that familiar depression creeping up on him as he contemplated the situation. For the first half of class, he sat writing in the journal that he always carried with him, feeling like no one, not even Adam, could possibly understand.

The scene flashed through his mind in a matter of seconds. All he said aloud to Erik was, "I don't know. I just can't seem to get happy and stay happy. Except when you're around." Jeremy grabbed Erik and held him tight.

It was on the brink of getting dark when they heard a horn honk. Erik thrust Jeremy away from his body and jumped backwards. They turned and saw Adam's Bronco waiting in the parking lot.

"Whew! I thought we were busted for sure."

"You want a ride home?"

"Yeah, I better," Erik said.

They rode in silence until they were a few blocks from Erik's house. "Drop me off here, okay? I'm supposed to be out running."

"Call me later," Jeremy said.

Erik circled his block a few times to break a sweat before he went home. All the while he kept hearing Jeremy's words: "I just keep wondering how we're going to make it through...."

Chapter Nine

Isabelle took her seat as the applause died down. She set the crinkled script down on her desk and stared at it as her classmates complimented her performance. Her heart thumped against her ribs, accompanying the adrenaline coursing through her veins. "So this is what Meg meant," she thought. "I could get addicted to this."

Half-listening to the other students as they read their scenes, Isabelle couldn't wait to hear what Mr. Kinney thought of her existential love story. When the last student stepped offstage, Mr. Kinney stood up and faced the class.

"Nice work, my friends. Some of you are really getting it. Excellent job for a first script and performance. I look forward to seeing more," their teacher praised the class. "Now I will give individual feedback. While I'm consulting with each student, I want the rest of you to work on your next scene."

"What's the topic?" someone called out.

"Let the topic choose you," he answered.

"Duh, we should know him by now," a girl next to Isabelle said.

Juiced from her first foray on stage, Isabelle struck the paper with her pen without delay. She scribbled a few details to set the scene and then began the dialogue. The scene involved six characters standing in a circle. They were different ages, races, and religions. As each one began to speak, one of the other characters interrupted to give their opinion on who he or she thought that character was. No one in the circle was able to define him or herself without someone else interrupting. At the height of the scene, Isabelle heard her name being called.

She looked up and saw Mr. Kinney signaling her over. Isabelle turned her paper over and set the pen down in the middle of it, before joining her teacher. She sat down next to him and kicked her heels against the stage while she waited for him to begin.

"Isabelle, tell me about your scene."

"Uh, what do you want me to say about it?"

"What does it mean to you?"

"I guess it was just what was on my mind when you gave us the assignment. It's on the short side," Isabelle apologized. "And not very deep."

"Not deep? Of course it's deep. Your simplicity makes it deep."

"Yeah okay." Isabelle fiddled with a paper clip.

"Your writing is strong and your sense of character is good, but you held back onstage." Mr. Kinney said it like he was asking a question.

"Well, I've never performed for an audience before. I thought they might think it was stupid. But then when I started, it felt pretty good."

"You'll get more and more comfortable as you do this. I think you'll be a great playwright one day. I'm guessing you enjoy the writing more than the acting, yes?"

"I'm definitely more at home with pen and paper than expressing it out loud."

"What is your new scene about?"

"You'll see. It's still in the fetal stage."

"Well, I have no doubt it'll be interesting."

Isabelle returned to her desk and turned her paper back over. Even after class ended, she remained in place, tossing words onto the page while Mr. Kinney graded student scripts at his desk. Neither of them spoke until Mr. Kinney looked at the clock and said, "It's four o'clock. Time to get back to the real world."

Isabelle folded her papers and put them into her notebook. She stopped at the edge of his desk and said, "I think I'm falling in love, Mr. Kinney."

He folded his hands and looked at his protégé. "With?"

She winked at him and smiled.

"Do I dare ask again?"

Isabelle leaned over and whispered, "Theater."

A smile turned up the edges of his lips. "Don't let her break your heart."

Isabelle laughed. "I'll try not to."

"Just for the record..." he started. "She will eventually. But you'll still love her."

"Thanks for letting me stay late."

Isabelle walked out into the empty courtyard and realized that she'd completely forgotten about meeting Maxine after school. Maxine had been hinting about a surprise adventure she wanted to take Isabelle on. But now she was nowhere in sight. Isabelle sighed. "I'm going to have to make this up to her big."

Trying not to be upset at Isabelle's no-show, Maxine sat on the bus to Lake Park. When she exited at the Front St. stop, Maxine got out the directions she'd printed off Mapquest to get her bearings. It didn't take her long to find herself standing under a sign reading: Outbooks.

Once there, however, she wasn't sure that she wanted to go in. "What if people think I'm gay?" Even if nobody in Lake Park knew Maxine, she still didn't want to risk being seen there. "Come on, I've made it this far," she pepped talked herself as she opened the door.

A bell jingled in her arrival and Maxine ducked into the first aisle she saw. She bent down and pretended to know exactly what she was looking for. As her heartbeat slowed down, she focused on the titles in front of her and read the tiny sign on the shelf: *Gay Male Erotica*. Maxine scooted around the corner, glancing at the titles for a section that was safer to be caught in.

"Can I help you find something?" a man across the store called out. Maxine turned around and mumbled, "Um, not really. I'm just browsing."

"Well, browse all you want. You don't even have to *buy* anything. See those couches over there? Get yourself a cup of coffee and make yourself at home."

His words did make her feel more at ease, so she stood up straight and looked over the shelves at the rest of the store. Maxine made her way into a hallway that led to a patio out back. Covering the hallway walls were postcards, flyers, and newspaper clippings. Maxine must have been standing in the same place for fifteen minutes reading the wall, when someone said, "Is that *you*, Max?"

"Huh?" She jumped. "Jeremy!"

"Hey girl, what are you doing in my neck of the woods?" Jeremy hopped from one foot to the other.

"I just found this place on the Internet and it looked cool, so I took the bus over."

"What do you think?"

"At first I was kind of nervous coming in here," she admitted. "But I like it. I can't believe how much cool stuff they have."

"Yeah, this place is like my second home. Did you meet Matthew? He's one of the owners."

"Is that him?"

"No, that's his partner, Joshua. Matthew's the guy behind the coffee bar." Jeremy pointed. "They've owned this place for twenty years together. You have to hear their stories!"

"I'd love to."

"Where's your other half?" Jeremy asked.

"Flaked on me," Maxine answered.

"Bummer. Still fighting that chemistry, huh?"

"Who knows? Maybe it's just chemistry on my part."

"Just for the record—Erik thinks she likes you, too, but is still freaked out because of the Mandy thing."

Maxine turned back to the flyers on the walls. "There's so much going on. I didn't even know that there were groups like these that people could go to. Look at these flyers: Lesbian Parenting Group, Gay Fiction Book Club, Co-Dependents Anonymous, Women's Mystery Night... there's something for everyone."

"Yeah, we should check some of them out. I've been trying to convince the guys to start a teen book group, but they're a little afraid of being attacked as 'recruiters'," Jeremy explained.

Maxine flipped open her notebook and said, "I'm going to call some of these numbers. There's not much on here for people our age, though."

"What about this?" Jeremy pointed to a bright yellow flyer near the back door. He read it aloud:

> **Think you're the only one out there? Want to meet other GLBT teenagers? Come to a meeting for GLBTQ youth ages 13-19 at the MCC Church on 7th St. Saturday October 27th, 7-9 pm. No drugs or alcohol.**

Maxine wrote down the phone number and circled it three times. "Do you think they'd go with us?"

"I don't see why not. Of course, Erik will have to concoct some crazy story to get out of the house," Jeremy added. "But we should definitely invite them anyway."

"I think it'd be so much fun. Do you think other kids will really go?"

"I don't know. Maybe we should help publicize it." He pulled the flyer off the wall and brought it up to Matthew. "Can we make some photocopies of this?"

"Lemme see," Matthew said, sliding his glasses down his nose. "Tell you what, I'll go make two copies and you can make more later if you want."

"Thanks, Matt. We just want to make sure everyone finds out about this."

"Well, not *every*one, Jeremy. Be careful whom you give it to. You don't want to stir up the Fundies."

"But it's *at* a church," Maxine said. "Wouldn't that be on the hypocritical side?"

"Ah, therein lies the irony," Matthew said.

"If Christians hate gay people so much, then why would a church hold a meeting for us?" she asked.

"Oh, not MCC. It's actually a gay-friendly Christian church," he explained.

"My parents don't go to church, but I don't think they would care if I went." Maxine tried to imagine Isabelle setting foot in a church.

"This may be a good way to check it out," Jeremy said, waving the flyer in front of her.

"Well, I better get going. It's going to take me awhile to get home."

"I'm so glad I saw you here!" Jeremy gave Maxine a hug. "Next time bring Erik with you, okay?"

"Drag him, you mean?"

"Ugh. Don't even go there."

Maxine made her way to the door and waved goodbye to Matthew and Joshua. "Thanks for the hospitality."

"Sure sweetie. Come back anytime."

"I plan to." Maxine let the door shut and retraced her steps to the bus stop, not caring who might see her.

Chapter Ten

The next weeks sped by as they came to the final days leading up the charity run. Isabelle and Maxine continued their dance of "I like you, but I'm scared of liking you" while Erik submerged himself in plans for the race.

Erik stood outside the Principal's office with a trembling finger hovering over the intercom button. "Go ahead," Mr. Martinez prompted.

"Good morning," Erik began. "We'll be hosting the first annual charity run from Foresthill to Lake Park this Saturday, October 13th. The proceeds will go to Arts for Kids—an organization that exposes inner-city kids to fine art. Our final meeting will be in room 515 after school tomorrow, so come on by."

"Nice job, Erik," Mr. Martinez stated. "I think you may put Foresthill High on the map."

Erik walked down the hallway to his second period class, wondering if he'd bitten off more than he could chew. The race was now just two days away and there were many details yet to be worked out.

"Hey Erik, what's up?" Mark called from a few feet away. "I heard you on the loudspeaker."

"Yeah, we've only got a couple days left to pull this thing together. I'm still gathering volunteers."

"I can help if you want. You said you needed people to hand out water and stuff, right?" Mark offered.

"Thanks. Then I'll see you at the meeting tomorrow?"

"Yep, I'll be there." Mark sauntered down the hallway, tossing his bathroom pass in the air.

Every head turned when Erik walked into the classroom. "Sorry I'm late," he whispered to the teacher.

"I know—we all heard you," Mrs. Angelini cut him off. "Just get started on your quiz."

Erik sat down and pulled out a pencil. But after writing his name on the quiz, he froze up. Usually an effortless math student, Erik stared at the numbers on the page like he'd never seen them before. He took a deep breath and closed his eyes. "Pull it together," he told himself. He tried to clear his mind and focus on the paper on his desk.

"Time's up. Turn in your quizzes," his teacher instructed fifteen minutes later, her voice jolting Erik out of his daydreams. He had made no other marks than his name on the top. Not making eye contact with Mrs. Angelini, he shoved it into the middle of the pile.

For the rest of the class period, Erik tried to pay extra attention to the trig lesson, but was relieved when the bell finally rang. The rest of the day passed in a similar manner and Erik was glad when it was time for cross-country practice. "It must just be the stress of pulling this thing together," he thought, as he stretched his hamstrings.

"Where are we running today?" Erik asked his coach.

"The Valley Mile."

"See you up there!" Erik took off before the rest of the team finished their warm-ups.

He started at a pace that he couldn't maintain for the distance, but didn't slow down until he was sure that he was far ahead of the pack. Alone, Erik resumed the monologue in his mind. "What's the deal with Mark? Why does he bug me so much? I should be happy that he wants to help out. But he gets on my nerves, like I should just forget he hung out with Jacob Schmidt and made my life hell last year."

The Valley Mile was right next to the middle school football field, and Erik had just begun to descend into its shady depths when he heard cheering. He stopped and saw his high school's football team running onto the field, flanked by Foresthill High cheerleaders. "What are they doing here?" he wondered and then remembered that their home field was still being drained from a broken water main earlier that week.

Leaning against a tree, Erik watched the troops drop to their hands as their coach barked out orders. Padded and helmeted, they all looked alike, but Erik found himself seeking out Mark anyway. Forcing himself to stop staring at the toned male bodies, he glanced over at the cheerleaders practicing their kicks on the sidelines. He spotted Mandy and almost waved. Then, seeing a pack of fellow runners ascending the hill, he pushed himself off the tree and sped into the canyon.

As he ran, Erik continued to grapple with his thoughts. He jumped from thinking about Mark to Jeremy to the charity run to Mandy to Isabelle and back to Mark again. Unaware of time passing, Erik emerged from the canyon and was on his way back down the hill before he even realized that he was almost done with practice.

Arriving home with just a few minutes to spare before dinner, Erik washed up and joined his mother in the kitchen. His father was out of town on a military consulting job and the house had been quiet for days. Though loquacious in his own mind, Erik barely spoke to his mother throughout the meal. The television in the background provided the only relief from silence.

Towards midnight, Erik closed his eyes and listened to the quiet in the house. Living there with just his mother was almost like living alone. Every so often he could hear her slinking around the rooms whispering. She reminded him of the woman in the story "The Yellow Wallpaper", in which the protagonist slowly lost her mind because of her indifferent husband. At the end of the story, the woman locked her husband out of the room and tore all of the wallpaper off the bedroom walls in order to free the women trapped behind it. Erik listened for signs of impending insanity as his mother crept about.

Erik set his chin in his palm and brought his attention back to tomorrow's tasks. Within moments, he was asleep. The ringing phone woke him up at three a.m. His head bolted up, causing a cramp to shoot through his neck. Rubbing the sore spot, he answered the phone with a whisper. "Hello?"

"Erik. It's me."

"Jeremy? What's wrong? Why do you sound so far away?" Erik was fully awake now.

"I'm at the gas station. I didn't know where else to go."

"What happened? Are you by yourself?"

"I came out to my parents," Jeremy said. "They weren't too happy about it."

"Did they kick you out?"

"Not exactly. But they made it clear that I had to go to counseling in order to cure me of it."

"Cure you? Is that possible?"

"I doubt it. I just had to get away, though. When I told them, my father got out a Bible and picked out all of these choice passages about how I'm going to hell if I'm gay. I laid in bed thinking about it and I had to get out of there. I just didn't want to face them in the morning."

"Oh man," Erik groaned. "What are you going to do?"

"I don't know. That's why I called you."

Erik paused for a moment. "What gas station? Is there a way for you to get over here?"

"Just a few blocks from home," Jeremy answered. "Maybe I can hitch a ride over to Foresthill."

"Isn't that a little dangerous? Especially at this hour."

"Well, what choice do I have? *You* can't come get me, can you?"

For a moment Erik considered taking the car but knew that there was no way he could get away with it, even with his father out of town. "Can you call Adam?"

"I'll try," Jeremy said.

Before Erik could say anything else, the phone went dead. He rubbed his eyes and looked at the clock. For the next twenty minutes he paced back and forth holding the phone in his hand. Every few minutes he'd turn it on to check for a dial tone. "Damn, I should have taken the car," he said. "God only knows where he is now."

After Adam and Erik had both failed him, Jeremy sat on the curb wondering what to do. The only cars that stopped at the gas station at this late hour possessed unsavory types whom Jeremy knew better than to tangle with. Before leaving the gas station, however, he was able to shoulder-tap a young man cruising by on a bike to get him some alcohol.

He wrapped the bottle in a sweatshirt and shoved it into his backpack. Dusting off the back of his pants, Jeremy checked his wallet for cab fare. After spending most of his money on the liquor, he realized that he didn't have enough for the ride across the river to Erik's house. He looked at his watch, slung his backpack onto his shoulders, and began his journey.

As he walked, he replayed the scene with his parents. After he and Maxine had met at Outbooks, something in him shifted. When he had returned home that afternoon, he pinned the flyer for the GLBTQ youth meeting on his bedroom wall right above his desk. It served as a beacon of hope, a confirmation that it was all right to be gay. It remained there, helping Jeremy garner the courage to tell his parents.

"Mom, Dad, I have something to tell you." Jeremy had waited until dinner was almost over before spitting out those words.

"What is it honey?" his mother asked.

Jeremy coughed and then blurted out, "I'm gay."

Their smiles froze.

"You're what?" His father cocked his head as if he hadn't heard correctly.

"I've been trying to figure out how to tell you. But I'm gay," Jeremy repeated.

At that admission, his mother burst into tears. "No you're not. You're just confused."

"Mom, don't cry. It's okay. I'm okay. I'm still me." Jeremy tried to console her.

"Son, I think you need to see something before you go around claiming this, uh, preference," his father stated. He left the room and soon returned with a Bible, which he plunked down in front of Jeremy. Thumbing through it, he picked out a few choice passages that his pastor had elaborated on many times in his sermons. Jeremy shrunk down in his chair as he listened.

"But I thought that Jesus loves everyone. No matter what," Jeremy recalled from his Sunday school lessons.

"Only if you repent of your sins, Jeremy. Otherwise you are going to Hell," his father declared. "If you continue to have homosexual thoughts you will be condemned."

"But..." Jeremy tried to defend himself. This hadn't gone exactly as planned. "I can't help it. It's just the way I was born."

His mother's sobs escalated into howls. "This is my fault? How dare you blame me!"

"I'm not blaming you for anything, Mom. I've always been gay—I'm just telling you about it now."

"We're putting you in counseling at the church. I think they have a group for people who've been led astray," his father spoke. "Don't worry. We can handle this. You'll soon be cured, son."

Jeremy sighed. "Well, I'm gonna go to my room now. I'm really tired."

His parents looked at their gay son and then at each other. "Jeremy, we still love you," his mother said. "Just get a good night's sleep. It'll be better in the morning."

His father added, "I'll call Pastor Robbins tomorrow. You're going to be okay, Jeremy. I'm just glad we caught this early on."

Jeremy nodded and returned to his room. As soon as he shut the door he began packing. The wall of depression that he'd always been able to see over now blocked his view. He didn't see any alternative but to run away. Unpinning the flyer from his bulletin board, Jeremy folded it into his journal. Then he got into bed and waited. When the house was finally silent, he slid up the sash window and jumped to the ground.

Nearing the bridge to Foresthill, Jeremy stopped and readjusted his backpack. He looked back towards his home in Lake Park and then looked towards Erik's house. Without another moment's hesitation, he began the ascent of the mile-long bridge. When he reached the apex, Jeremy stopped again and dropped his backpack on the footpath. He leaned his arms on the railing and let the tears he'd been holding back fall into the river below. His incessant cries of "Why? Why? Why?" were drowned out by the rushing water.

Physically weakened, Jeremy's legs gave way and he fell to the ground. There he lay, convulsing in the emotional pain trapped in his body for so long. Every cry released a muscle spasm, until his body lay limp. Jeremy pushed himself upright into a seated position and dangled his feet through the guardrails over the river. Uncapping the bottle that lay in his bag, Jeremy gulped down the acrid substance. He returned the half-empty bottle back to his bag and stared out over the water.

For over an hour, Jeremy sat on the bridge, unaware of how cold his body had grown. He thought about his life, his parents, his friends, and his one true love. "I could do it if I didn't have Erik," he concluded. "None of the rest of those things matter."

"But then again, how much does Erik really love me? Or even care? He didn't even try to come and get me. Nobody really cares." Jeremy teetered on the brink. "But, there isn't much he could do. I guess there's nothing anyone can do."

Jeremy pulled himself up and leaned over the railing. He looked up at the scaffolding that rose up from the concrete road and let his mind wander. "It would be over fast. No mess for anyone to clean up." As he began to consider the option, Jeremy gained strength. His muscles geared for action and his thoughts were clear. "I better leave a note," he decided. "Or Erik will never forgive me."

He squatted down and rifled through his backpack for a pen and his journal. Jeremy knew there was no right way to say goodbye, but he also knew that he couldn't leave Erik forever wondering.

Dear Erik,

First of all, I'm sorry. I know you're going to be furious with me, but believe me when I tell you that I had no other choice. I have disappointed everyone. My parents and God, especially. And I don't want to drag you down with me. So, trust me when I tell you that this is the right decision. I love you and wish that there could have been some other way. But I don't know of any, so this is what I have to do. Don't ever forget me. You're the only thing worth living for, and if I can't be with you, then life is not worth living.

Eternally yours, Jeremy

Jeremy capped the pen and closed the book. Shoving his fear to the depths of his stomach, he placed a foot on the metal railing and climbed up the scaffolding. He kept his eyes focused on the steps above him until he was twenty feet above the street.

Holding onto a thick cable, Jeremy swayed a little when he first looked down at the water. His balance grew steadier as he fastened his gaze on the horizon, where the sun was just peeking over the water. The day was dawning and cars were starting to cross the bridge. Hidden behind a steel post, the only evidence of Jeremy was his backpack lying on the ground.

Little did Jeremy know that Erik was still up holding a vigil for him just a few miles away. He stayed on his knees praying, "Oh God, please protect him. I'll do anything, God. Oh, God don't let anything happen to him," over and over again. Erik's prayers calmed him, as he knew there was nothing else that he could do.

Jeremy, wavering on the decision between life and death, suddenly felt a great sense of peace. It was as though the reality of his life wasn't a reality anymore. The only thing in his consciousness was the deep river below him and the sun bringing light into the sleeping town. It didn't matter what his parents thought. It didn't matter what the church thought. It didn't matter even what he thought. It was the image of Erik at his funeral that broke Jeremy's resolve. "I can't do this to him," he said. "It's just not fair."

More carefully than he climbed up, Jeremy scaled down the scaffolding on shaky legs. Once on solid ground, the gravity of what he had been ready to do seized his stomach and Jeremy threw up over the railing into the water. Over and over he retched until his body sank into exhaustion. When he recovered enough to walk, Jeremy heaved his backpack over his shoulders and shuffled toward Erik's house.

Chapter Eleven

Jeremy squatted in the shrubbery outside until he saw Erik emerge. "Hey," he whispered, as Erik strode down his front path.

"Oh my God!" Erik tripped over a rock and almost joined Jeremy in the bushes. "How did you get here?"

"It's a long story. Can I come in?"

"I'm on my way to school. What would I tell my mother?" Erik reached out his hands to Jeremy.

"Just sneak me in. I'm so dead tired that I won't move from your bed. I'll even sleep in your closet if you want me to. Please Erik? I'm desperate."

Erik looked at Jeremy's disheveled appearance. "Hold on, I have an idea. Come with me." He led Jeremy by the arm down the block and then up a crooked path to a front door. He knocked and waited. When they heard footsteps Erik squeezed Jeremy's hand once and then let it go.

"Hi Mr. Foxfire," Erik said. "I have a huge favor to ask of you."

Isabelle's father looked at Erik's companion and said, "Okay. What's up?"

"This is Jeremy. He's my...friend. You know? His parents freaked out on him last night and he had to leave home. I know it's a lot to ask, but can he stay here today until I'm done with school? He's been out all night and has no place to go."

"Are you okay?" Mr. Foxfire asked the glassy-eyed boy reeling in front of him. Jeremy shook his head and burst into tears. Isabelle's father reached out and cupped his hand under Jeremy's elbow and led him inside.

Seated at the kitchen table with a cup of hot tea warming his hands, Jeremy told Mr. Foxfire the short version of the last twenty-four hours of his life. He left out the scene on the bridge, however.

When he was finished, Mr. Foxfire said, "You can stay here, but I want you to call your parents and let them know you're safe. You don't have to tell them precisely where you are, but they deserve to know you're alive."

Jeremy's skin crawled when he thought about how close to not being alive he had come just a few hours earlier. "Okay," he agreed, and accepted the phone Mr. Foxfire extended to him. "Erik and I will give you some privacy." They exited the room.

Isabelle met them in the hallway and said, "What's going on?"

"I'll explain on the way to school," Erik answered. "We better get going."

All day long, Erik thought about Jeremy and could barely wait until his classes were over so he could see him again. As soon as the last bell rang, however, he forced himself into business mode and trotted over to room 515 where students were already gathering. Soon the room was packed with over forty students and faculty who'd volunteered to help with the charity race. Even Mr.

Martinez poked his head in the room and gave Erik a thumbs up sign.

"Thank you for coming. This is a major event and we can use all the help we can get. But just think about how many kids we'll be helping." Erik paused as the group broke out into cheers.

When the voices died down, Erik continued. "This is how it's going to work. I'm going to pass around a sign up sheet so you can pick whatever task you want to do." After some chaos, the volunteers divided and committed themselves to their duties.

In the midst of it all, Isabelle walked into the room unnoticed by everyone but Maxine. She stopped mid-sentence and fixed her eyes on the glow coming through the doorway. Isabelle glided through the crowd, leading Jeremy by the hand towards Erik who was commanding a group of gophers like a Fortune 500 CEO.

Standing behind him, Isabelle barked, "Sir, yes sir!"

Erik spun around. "Just in time. I need you two."

"Well, put us to work then," Jeremy said.

Sitting at a nearby desk, Mark turned his head so he could listen to their conversation. He pretended to be making a list, but his eyes were really on Jeremy. He tried to jog his memory of where he'd seen him before. "I'm pretty sure he doesn't go here," he thought. "Lakepark High, maybe?"

"Why don't you help me out?" Erik said to Jeremy. "And Isabelle can work with Maxine."

"Maxie!" she yelled from across the room. "I'm at your beck and call."

"Well, it's about time!"

"What do you want me to do?"

"You can help me get entry forms numbered."

Isabelle fell into line next to Maxine. "What are you doing after all of this is over? Want to spend the night?"

"I'll ask my parents."

They worked long into the evening, their numbers thinning as the hours passed. At 9 p.m., Erik announced, "All right everyone. We're not quite finished, but we have to stop for tonight. If anyone can show up an hour early tomorrow, we can take care of the last minute details. Raise your hand if you think you can make it."

About a dozen people raised their hands. "Okay then, how about 6 a.m. at the starting line?"

"I'll come early," Mark said to Erik before he walked out. "Have a good night."

Jeremy looked at him and then at Erik. "Who's that?"

"Oh, just a guy from my history class last year," Erik answered and began to tidy the area around him. "All right, I'm ready. Let's get out of here."

"All night he kept looking over here at us. Are you friends with him?"

"More like acquaintances. Nobody important."

"It just seemed like he was watching you."

"Not that I know of." Erik brushed it off.

"How are you getting home?" Isabelle asked Maxine as they walked out of the building, followed by the boys.

"I called my mom a few minutes ago. She'll be here fairly soon."

"We'll wait with you, right guys?" Isabelle called back to Erik and Jeremy. They were still engaged in a hushed conversation, but nodded in acknowledgment.

Isabelle sat next to Maxine on a low stone wall in front of the school. "I would invite you to stay over tonight," Isabelle said. "But I've kind of got company. Jeremy's in trouble at home. Poor guy."

"That's all right. Saturday's better anyway—we have to get up so dang early for the race tomorrow morning."

"Well, if I had it my way, you could stay over both nights." Isabelle played with her pigtails as she talked.

"Me too," Maxine said.

Maxine's mother pulled up to the curb. "See you at six, okay?" Isabelle said. "Come on boys, stop your lovey-dovey stuff and let's get home."

As they began to walk down the sidewalk, Maxine's mother pulled up along side of the trio. She rolled down her window and called, "You kids want a ride?"

"That's okay, we'll walk," Erik answered.

"*You* can walk. I'm getting a ride!" Isabelle said. "See you at home, Jeremy." She jumped into the backseat.

"Mom, Isabelle wants me to spend the night tomorrow, can I?" Maxine twisted around in the front seat to face Isabelle.

"Why don't you two stay at our house instead? That pregnant cow of yours could use some company—I think she's about ready to calve," her mother said.

"We could, I guess," Maxine said. "It's still warm enough to sleep out in the barn if we wanted to."

"Yeah, that'd be more fun," Isabelle agreed. "I love it at your place, Mrs. Kotamo. All those animals are like heaven to me."

"Well, you'll certainly get your fill if you sleep in the barn." Mrs. Kotamo pulled up to the curb and dropped Isabelle off.

"See you in the morning, Max. Thanks for the ride."

Erik and Jeremy strolled back to Isabelle's house, relieved to have a chance to talk. In the darkness of the night, the boys let their arms brush each other's, sometimes linking fingers for a moment or two. Whenever they heard a car in the distance, they stepped apart and waited for it to pass.

"Finally, we're alone," Erik said. "I've been going crazy today. Tell me what's going on, Jeremy."

"I told you last night. My parents wigged out, so I had to get out," Jeremy replied. "I couldn't get a ride so I walked to your house."

Erik attempted the math in his head. "I know it's a long way, but you called me from the gas station at three a.m. and you got to my house at seven. Were you walking that entire time?"

"Not the whole time. I sat on the bridge for quite awhile just thinking."

"Weren't you scared?"

"A little bit. But I was mostly so upset about everything at home that I didn't have time to be scared."

"Well, I'm just glad you're safe. I don't want to lose you, you know?"

"Nothing's permanent, Erik," Jeremy said.

"What do you mean?"

"Nothing. Just that you can't really count on people to be the way you want them to be."

"Are you talking about me?"

"No. All I'm saying is that we sometimes just have to live with life being a little less perfect than we want it to be," Jeremy explained.

"I thought you believed that we could control our own destiny. What's changed?"

"I'm not sure. I just don't live under the illusion that things are automatically going to be okay."

"So what now? Does this change things between us?" He had never heard Jeremy speak with such resignation.

Jeremy scuffed the curb in front of Isabelle's house with his tennis shoe. "Erik, I love you. I don't want things to change between us. But things are different for me now. I have to be realistic. I don't even know where I'm going to go. Isabelle's family is great, but they aren't going to let me live there forever."

Erik thought for a few seconds and came up with no other solutions, so he remained silent.

"See what I mean?" Jeremy said. "There's not much to be hopeful about."

"I wish I could help."

"You do help. Just by being here." He hugged Erik and said, "Get some rest. I'll see you in the morning."

"Goodnight," Erik whispered and walked the rest of the way home alone. For the next two blocks, he pushed his tired brain to think of some solution to help Jeremy.

Succumbing to the day's emotional and physical trials, Erik flopped on his bed, clothes and all, and fell asleep. He spent a night of dreamless sleep, but when he woke in the morning, Erik brushed his cheeks and found them damp. Pressing on his puffy eyes, Erik rolled out of bed and dropped onto the floor. After plugging through fifteen push-ups, Erik dressed and headed towards Isabelle's house to escort his sleepy comrades to the starting line.

Chapter Twelve

As promised, the volunteers clustered around Erik for their instructions at dawn and when the starting shot was fired, everyone was in place along the race route. Once the pack of runners left the starting line on Foresthill High's track, Erik breathed easier. The day held a perfect autumn crispness as the rising sun tingled the runners' skin. Watching the hundreds of legs dart by made Erik wish he was out there, instead of holding a clipboard at his side. On his other side, however, stood Jeremy.

Erik looked at him and smiled. "We did it. I can't believe we pulled this off."

"You're good, Erik. Didn't doubt you for a second," Jeremy said.

"Thanks. You're a pretty fine inspiration."

Jeremy whispered something in return that made Erik blush. Erik was relieved to find Jeremy in an upbeat mood this morning.

Across the field, Mark packed water bottles into a duffle bag and heaved it over his shoulder. With his free hand, he waved to Erik and headed to deliver the reinforcements to the volunteers on the bridge. Erik nodded in return and turned back to Jeremy. "Let's clean up here and get over to the finish line."

Meanwhile, Isabelle and Maxine were stationed at the summit of the bridge, marking the halfway point of the race. They tossed out water and shouted encouraging words to the runners as they passed by.

Isabelle entertained herself by chanting silly rhymes. "Run your buns, you're almost done." She jogged in place.

"Move those muscles, put on that hustle." She slapped her thighs.

"If you get to the line before nine, you'll get to dine at Pancake Pines." She simulated eating breakfast.

Maxine rolled her eyes at the last cheer. "All right. That's a little much, Izzy."

Mark stood a few yards away from the girls for quite awhile before talking to them. When he saw them break apart from one of their many huddles, he walked over. "Hi, I'm Mark."

"Isabelle. Thanks for delivering the water." She stuck out her hand.

"No prob. I'm happy to be here. This is a great thing you guys put together."

Maxine looked at the tall, muscular boy standing next to her. "I'm Maxine."

"Yeah, I've seen you around," Mark said.

Isabelle squinted at him. "Don't you hang out with Jacob Schmidt?"

"Used to. Not anymore. I didn't realize what an ass he was until last year."

"No offense. But you seem like a nice guy. What the hell were you thinking?" Isabelle made a sour face.

"Not much apparently." Mark smiled. "Can I just blame it on being a stupid freshman?"

"Give him a break, Isabelle," Maxine said. "We all make mistakes in judgment sometimes, right?"

"Yeah, I guess. All right, Mark. We'll let you slide."

"You and Erik are tight, huh?"

"Since Kindergarten. Why?" Isabelle replied.

"No reason. I don't know him very well, but he seems like a cool guy."

"Erik's the best."

"Anyway, it's nice to meet you. I better get back to doing my job."

As he walked back to his post, Isabelle said, "I wonder what that was all about."

"Yeah, it was kinda odd." Maxine watched Mark dig through his bag for the remaining bottles of water.

"Whatever. It looks like this is the last of them." Isabelle pointed to the few stragglers peaking the bridge. "Let's head toward the finish line." She unhooked their bikes from the mesh fence and hopped on. Maxine followed Isabelle's lead and cruised the remaining few miles along side of the runners.

When they got to the finish line, Isabelle's back wheel skidded into a stop. "Who invited *them*?"

Maxine looked in the direction of Isabelle's outstretched thumb. Foresthill High's cheerleading squad framed the finish line, rooting for each participant that crossed over. Mandy's voice echoed across the intersection. Unable to look away, Isabelle's stare grabbed Mandy's attention. Her eyes fixed on Isabelle's as her voice rose in celebration of the runners. After not speaking for nearly six months, the girls engaged in a long distance conversation.

Isabelle's gaze raged across the street. "How dare you invade my territory?"

Mandy's replied coolly, "But aren't we here for the same reasons?"

"I know what my reasons are. What are yours?" Isabelle flashed back.

Mandy's eyes misted. "I just want things to be okay between us. Will you ever forgive me?"

Isabelle's head was caught between a nod and a shake. She broke the gaze and got off her bike. "Come on, Max. Let's find Erik."

"Are you okay?"

"It's a free country," she answered.

Uncertain whether to press her about Mandy, Maxine said, "There he is."

They walked their bikes over to where Erik was standing. "What's the word?" she asked.

He shuffled a stack of papers. "I think we raised over a thousand dollars."

"Awesome! How do you feel?" Isabelle asked.

"Excited. And relieved. I'm glad we did this, but also glad it's almost over," Erik answered.

"That makes two of us! Let's make a pact to not make any more pacts this year."

"You got it."

"Well, I think we're going to head home now," Isabelle said. "You've got the clean up crew set, right?"

"Yeah, go ahead. Get a nap. I know you must be as wiped out as I am."

"Can Jeremy stay with you tonight? I'm going to spend the night at Maxine's."

Before Erik could answer, Jeremy interjected, "Definitely."

"Okay, well that's settled. We're outta here." Isabelle rolled her bike off the sidewalk. The girls pushed their bikes a few more feet when a truck pulled up beside them.

"You want to throw your bikes in the back?" someone called out the window.

Isabelle craned her neck and saw Mark's silhouette. She looked over at Maxine and said, "What the heck? I don't think he's an axe murderer and I'm beat."

Mark helped them lay their bikes down in the bed of the truck and took off over the now-empty bridge.

"Isn't that the guy from the meeting last night?" Jeremy observed.

"Yeah, I didn't realize Isabelle and Maxine knew him," Erik replied. "I guess they really didn't want to ride their bikes home."

Inside the truck, Isabelle echoed that sentiment. "Thanks so much. I can't imagine pedaling one more doggone block."

"How did you get your license already?" Maxine asked. "I thought you were a sophomore like us."

"My birthday was just last week," Mark answered. "My parents didn't want me to be one of the younger ones in my class so I stayed in preschool twice."

"I live way out in the sticks. Are you sure you don't mind driving us home?" Maxine gave him directions to the Kotamo ranch.

"Are you kidding? I've only had my license a week. I want to drive all the time!"

"That must make you pretty popular," Isabelle said. "In addition to being Mr. Quarterback and all."

"Popularity isn't all it's cracked up to be."

"I wouldn't know," Isabelle said.

"Hey, what do you think about hanging out sometime," Mark offered.

Isabelle looked at him with a strange expression. "What do you mean?"

"Hang out. You know. Erik could come along too, maybe. I think it'd be fun."

"Listen dude. If you think we're going to live out some kinky fantasy of yours..." Isabelle smashed Maxine into door handle.

"Chill out. I know you're a lesbian. I'm just trying to branch out and meet more people. I thought that maybe we had some things in common."

"What could we possibly have in common?" Isabelle asked, as Mark's engine idled in Maxine's driveway. "Are you a lesbian, too?"

"Forget I said anything," Mark mumbled.

"Isabelle, don't be mean." Maxine gave her a little shove. "Mark, we'd love to hang out with you sometime." She scribbled her phone number on the back of a flyer and handed it to him.

Isabelle said, "I'm sorry. I sometimes assume people are up to no good."

"I don't blame you for being on guard."

"Thanks for driving us way out here," Isabelle said. "Give us a call if you feel like it."

Once Mark was gone, Isabelle turned to Maxine. "What do you want to do?"

"I don't know," she answered. The two of them had spent many days and nights together during the summer but had not yet been in the position they were now. It was clear to everyone around them and to each other that their feelings had surpassed pure friendship and moved into a gray zone with unwritten rules.

"Let's go sit by the creek," Isabelle suggested.

"Sounds good." Maxine led the way through the overgrown brush surrounding the edges of their property.

As they dangled their feet in the chilly water, they talked about the race, their encounter with Mark, and then drifted onto the subject of Jeremy and Erik, before getting to the conversation that they both were avoiding and longing for.

Maxine took the lead. "So, what about us?"

Dipping her hands into the water, Isabelle replied, "What's there to say about us?"

"Well, we've psychoanalyzed all of our friends. Don't you think we should talk about us now?"

"Um...uh...hmm..." Isabelle shielded the setting sun from her eyes and watched the glow settling on Maxine's face. She was certain at that very moment that what she had felt for Mandy months ago paled in comparison. "I want to show you something."

Maxine cocked her head. "Well, it's about time."

Isabelle tossed a pebble into Maxine's lap. "I'm serious. Remember those scenes I wrote for Mr. Kinney's class?" Isabelle unzipped her bag and slid a few sheets of paper from her folder and handed them to Maxine.

Maxine read the first scene and said, "I love the way that you say so much with just a few words."

"Let me read the second scene aloud," Isabelle said.

Maxine handed the paper back and Isabelle scanned it before opening her mouth.

"An Existential Love Story"

Scene Two: Two people in a restaurant.

Person 1: Are you ready to order?
Person 2: Not yet. I don't know what I want.
Person 1: Do you want to share a meal?
Person 2: Do you?
Person 1: Only if you do.
Person 2: I don't know what I want.
Person 1: I do.

Person 2: *What?*
Person 1: *Salmon.*
Person 2: *There's plenty of fish in the sea.*
Person 1: *But I want salmon.*
Person 2: *Then salmon you should have.*
Person 1: *Is that what you want, too?*
Person 2: *Salmon's not bad.*
Person 1: *But is it good enough?*
Person 2: *For one meal? I think so.*
Person 1: *What if you had to eat it every day?*
Person 2: *I don't know if I could.*
Person 1: *What do you know about salmon?*
Person 2: *They swim, breed, and die.*
Person 1: *Exactly.*
Person 2: *So?*
Person 1: *We can eat salmon.*
Person 2: *Or not.*

Isabelle set the paper on her lap and picked up another pebble. "Well, what do you think?"

"I think you've got an incredible mind. A little neurotic, but incredible."

"I'm not fishing for compliments." Isabelle elbowed her friend.

"Thanks for sharing these with me. It does explain a lot about what's happening in your head."

"That's a relief."

Maxine watched Isabelle roll the papers into a tube. "It's me, Isabelle. You don't have to be scared. I'm your best friend."

"I know. I'm afraid of losing you," Isabelle admitted, leaving the "too" unspoken.

"Why would you lose me? Nothing is going to change how I feel about you."

Isabelle gulped. "And how is that?"

"Come on, Bella. You're not blind," Maxine said. "Are you gonna make me say it out loud?"

"Guess so." Isabelle smiled. "Or not. Maybe we just should leave it at that."

Ignoring her words, Maxine reached over and pulled the papers from Isabelle's fingers and twined them into her own. "Ever since we met last spring, I've felt very lucky to be your friend. But there's always been something unspoken that I just need to get out into the open." Isabelle's hands gripped Maxine's.

"I didn't say anything at first because you were going through so much with Mandy. And then you never mentioned those stupid notes I wrote you, so I just figured that our friendship was just going to stay that way forever," Maxine began. "But I have to tell you the truth, Iz. I have always had feelings towards you that go beyond friendship. And, now it's gotten too strong to pretend. I can only assume how you feel about me, but I'm not going to put words into your mouth. So...do you want to say anything?"

Isabelle hemmed and hawed before formulating an answer. "You're a lot braver than I am. Maxine, I can't even begin to tell you how you make me feel, because if I do, then it'll be out there, in the universe, and I won't be able to control it anymore."

"Whether you say it or not, it's still out there, Bella. Not admitting your feelings doesn't make them any less real," Maxine stated.

"I know. I just don't want to ruin things again. I couldn't stand it if I messed up our friendship. You think I lost it *last* year..."

"It's different with us," Maxine said. "I'm not Mandy, for one. And two, we are already best friends. We know each other, good and bad, and still love each other anyway. Don't you think that says something?"

"Yes, it does. I just don't want things to change."

"What if things changed for the better?"

"I could live with that."

"All right then. Put it out there. Tell me how you feel," Maxine insisted.

After months of holding back her feelings, Isabelle let the dam break. "I feel like I'm better with you than without you. And I just want to share everything I do and think with you. I just keep picturing us together, like we have a future. Like we're a couple."

Maxine kept nodding as she listened, a grin breaking her serious expression. "I have those fantasies, too."

"Max, how do you know that it's the right thing to do?"

"It just feels right. I'm not trying to pressure you. I just want us to be real with each other."

"Is it worth the risk?"

"Is anything worth the risk? I'd rather take a chance than never know what could have been. We can't just live in fear of what *might* happen." Maxine twisted her long hair into a bun and secured it with two sticks lying nearby.

"You look gorgeous," Isabelle said. "I don't think I've ever seen anyone as beautiful as you are."

Maxine leaned her head onto Isabelle's shoulder. "Amazing, isn't it?" she said, looking out at the unspoiled acres in front of them.

Isabelle didn't know if Maxine was referring to the scenery or to the way they were feeling, but answered "yes" to both.

Maxine tilted her head upwards to look at Isabelle. "It's all right," she said. "Everything's perfect." She snuggled closer to Isabelle's chest, reassuring that her words were true.

Chapter Thirteen

After a few moments of wondering what might happen next, Maxine jumped up. "Hey, I just remembered something that I've been *dying* to tell you! Come back to my room with me."

Isabelle stood up. "Are we having salmon?"

"Listen—you're going to be so excited. The other day I found this gay bookstore near where Jeremy lives—he was actually in the store the same time I was."

"Really? I didn't know we had anything like that within a hundred miles of here," Isabelle said, as they hurried toward the house.

"You might have known if you hadn't ditched me."

"I've apologized a hundred times for that!"

"Anyway, there was this wall full of flyers and—hold on, let me get it out of my backpack." She pulled out a wrinkled piece of paper and handed it to Isabelle.

Before Isabelle could even read it, Maxine blurted out, "It's a gay club! Cool huh? And it's just two weeks away."

"No way. Where is it?" Isabelle looked at the bottom of the flyer for an address. "MCC? What's that?"

"It stands for Metropolitan Community Church. Jeremy said that it's a gay-friendly church and its right there in Lake Park."

"Let me get this straight...a church is holding a gay club meeting? Has Hell frozen over?" Isabelle pretended to check out the window.

"Will you go with me? Please?" Maxine asked, draping her arms around Isabelle's neck. Isabelle reached up to pry the smoldering hands from her skin, but let her own hands rest on top of Maxine's when she got there.

"Yes," she answered. "I wouldn't miss it for the world."

To which, Maxine pulled her close and let her lips linger on Isabelle's until the room began to spin around them. Neither one of them inhaled or exhaled for the next thirty seconds. Maxine eventually pulled back and said, "You're the one, Isabelle. You know that, right?"

"I'm afraid I'm counting on it."

"Well, could you look a little happier about it?" Maxine tackled Isabelle onto the bed. "Let's make plans."

"Are Jeremy and Erik going?"

"I know Jeremy was going to ask him, but I don't know if he remembered, because of all the chaos going on at home and everything."

"Have you called the number?"

"Let's do it now!"

After just two rings, a voice answered; Isabelle slammed the phone down.

"What's wrong?" Maxine asked.

"Someone answered!"

"Uh, that's pretty typical when you dial a number..."

"I just got freaked out because I was expecting an answering machine. Shoot, now we can't call back."

"Let's just wait half an hour. Maybe they won't make the connection," Maxine said. "I have an idea about how to kill some time while we wait." She fluttered her lashes.

"Can I paint your nails?" Isabelle asked.

"Whatever floats your boat." Maxine lay back against a pile of pillows and allowed Isabelle to paint her toenails coral pink.

"Stop squirming! You're messing me up."

"I can't help it," Maxine protested. "You keep on tickling me!"

"Oh, honey, you don't even know what you've started!" Isabelle lunged for Maxine's ribs. She held her down and tickled her until Maxine cried for mercy. A few moments later, the two girls collapsed across Maxine's bed gasping for air between their giggles.

"Had enough?" Isabelle asked.

"You're ruthless."

"And you're a tease."

"A tease?" Maxine squealed. "What*ever* are you talking about?" She waggled her toes in Isabelle's face.

"Argh! You're driving me crazy!" Isabelle caught Maxine's foot and set it back down on the bed. "What am I going to do with you?"

"Anything you want, darling." Maxine flailed her arms wide open.

Isabelle jumped up and smoothed down her shirt. "Um, okay. We better make that call now."

Maxine propped herself up on an elbow. "If you can't stand the heat, get out of the kitchen."

Isabelle folded her arms across her chest.

"Okay. I'll stop. It's just so much fun to rattle your cage. Plus, you're so damn cute when you get flustered," Maxine taunted.

Isabelle growled. "Cute? Ugh!"

"You want a better word? How about gorgeous? Beautiful? Mind-blowing?"

"You're not helping." Isabelle threw a stuffed rabbit at Maxine's head and picked up the phone to redial.

This time, when someone answered, she said, "I have this flyer for a GLBTQ youth group meeting. Um, on October 27th."

"Oh, yes. Great! I'm so glad you saw the notice," the same woman with the Southern drawl answered.

"Can you tell me a little bit about it?" Isabelle asked.

"Well, most of the info is on the flyer, but I can tell you how to get here and what to expect," she replied. "I'm Reverend Kat, by the way."

"Reverend?" Isabelle repeated. She looked wide-eyed at Maxine.

"Yes, I'm the senior pastor."

"I didn't know women could be reverends."

"Things are a little different at our church. Women are welcome in the pulpit," Kat explained. "You should check out our 10 a.m. service tomorrow."

"I'm not much of the churchy type," Isabelle admitted. "No offense."

"None taken. I don't blame you, really. Most of us who came here have had bad experiences with churches. But then we found MCC."

"Is this club gonna be religious or something?"

Kat's laugh pealed over the phone line. "No, we just wanted to provide a safe and healthy place for gay and lesbian young people to meet and hang out."

"Sounds pretty cool. Do we need to RSVP or anything?" Isabelle asked.

"No, just show up at 7 pm. We'll have refreshments and some discussion topics. But after that first meeting, it'll all be on the group to figure out what they want to do."

"Thanks for the info," Isabelle said. "I guess I'll see you then, huh?"

"You bet. And feel free to come by any time you're in the neighborhood before then to introduce yourself. We have service tomorrow at 10 a.m.," Rev. Kat repeated.

Isabelle said goodbye and set the phone down in her lap. "What a trippy conversation," she said to Maxine. "That was the reverend—of the whole church—and she just talked to me like I was someone who mattered. She doesn't even know me."

"You do matter," Maxine said. "Haven't you ever been to church before?"

"Nope," Isabelle answered, then corrected herself. "Well, twice. I went with this girl I had a crush on in fifth grade. Her family was Catholic and I went with her after spending the night there a couple of times. It was *so* deathly boring!"

"My family doesn't really go to church, either," Maxine said. "But I kind of want to go. I don't know why, but I just have this curiosity."

"Well, Reverend Kat did invite me to tomorrow morning's service."

"Maybe we should. What harm could it do?"

"None, I guess. I just hate the idea of organized religion. It makes me think of those guys on TV screeching about us being sinners, damned to Hell."

"I say we go tomorrow."

"It's all the way out in Lake Park, isn't it?"

"We could get a ride. Hey, maybe Jeremy and Erik would want to go," Maxine said.

"If Erik agrees, I'm in," Isabelle decided, pretty sure that Erik wouldn't be allowed to go. She handed the phone to Maxine and let her make the call.

"Yes, we want to go!" Erik responded to the invitation. "But how are we going to get there?"

Jeremy, listening on the other line, said, "You know, Matthew and Joshua, the guys who run Outbooks, said that if I ever wanted to go, they'd pick me up."

"Do you think they'd come out to Foresthill to get us?"

He looked at his watch and said, "I think they're open 'til ten tonight. Let me call the store and we'll call you back in a minute."

Erik looked at his boyfriend chatting with Matthew on the phone. His smile indicated that they had procured a ride to church tomorrow. "He's perfect," Erik thought and reached over to hold Jeremy's hand. Jeremy played with his fingers while on the phone and Erik closed his eyes. "I can't believe he's here, lying in my bed right now."

"All right, we got a ride. How are we going to get out of the house tomorrow?" Jeremy asked.

"Just leave that up to me," Erik said. "Call the girls and tell them the details."

Chapter Fourteen

After his mother consented to their Sunday plan, Erik and Jeremy sat at opposite sides of the dining room table eating dinner. Erik couldn't remember the last time he saw his mother blush, but Jeremy had her giggling throughout the meal. By the time Erik mustered the courage to ask if Jeremy could spend the night, Mrs. Pennington had already offered.

When she saw Jeremy looking at his watch, she said, "You're welcome to stay here tonight, Jeremy. If it's okay with your parents."

"Thanks. I'd love to," he said. "Let me go call and see." Jeremy excused himself and went into the kitchen. He opened his wallet and pulled out Isabelle's number. "Hi Mom," he said to Mrs. Foxfire. "Can I spend the night over at Erik's?"

"Sure, honey. Be sure to call your own folks, too, okay?" Ana answered.

"Okay," Jeremy lied. "See you tomorrow."

Returning to the dining room, he said, "Thank you for such a wonderful meal, Mrs. Pennington. My mom said that I could stay over. I really appreciate your offer, Ma'am." He added a bow at the end.

Erik stifled a grin. "Come on Jeremy, let's find something to do."

"Have fun, boys," Marie said. "Let me know if you want dessert later."

"We will," Erik said. "By the way, can we use the computer tonight?"

"Sure. But don't stay online all night. I want the phone lines clear if your father calls."

Erik frowned. His father hadn't called in days. He felt a pang of guilt spring up in place of his secret happiness that his father wasn't around. "Don't worry, Mom. We're both pretty tired and will probably go to bed before long."

"I'll go set up the guest room," Marie said.

"Oh, don't go to any trouble for me. I'm fine sleeping on Erik's floor."

"No guest of ours is going to sleep on the floor," Marie insisted. "It's really not a hassle." She exited the room to pull fresh bedding out of the linen closet.

Erik and Jeremy went into Jack's office and shut the door. "Shoot," Erik said. "I didn't think about where you would sleep. That's clear across the house from my room."

"Well, I did. Actually, it's all I've been thinking about since dinner. We'll figure something out, all right?" Jeremy came up close and hugged Erik from behind.

Erik wiggled out of the embrace. "Not here," he whispered, looking at the walls filled with military memorabilia and exhibitions of manhood. He felt his father's eyes on him from every crevice of the room. "I wouldn't be surprised if this place was bugged."

Jeremy backed off. "What? I can't believe your father's that paranoid!"

"Well, he's high up in the military. It's part of his job to be suspicious."

"Let's go somewhere else, then," Jeremy said. "I don't really want to play on the computer. I just want to be close to you."

Erik thought for a minute, mentally surveying each room in the house and ranking its privacy capacity. "We could go out to my old tree house."

"You have a tree house? How cute."

"My brother and I built it together when I was younger. I haven't been up there in ages."

"All right. I'm up for adventure."

Erik grabbed a blanket off of his bed and a flashlight from the desk drawer; Jeremy brought his backpack. They crept out the back door and trod through the damp grass to a tree in the southwest corner of the yard. Cautiously climbing up the rotting ladder, Erik and Jeremy settled on the platform and spread the blanket out. For a few moments neither of them said anything.

Erik finally broke the silence and said, "I feel like a little kid being up here."

Jeremy leaned over and ran his hands across Erik's chest. "You don't feel like a little kid to me."

"I can't believe we're finally truly alone."

"I thought we'd never get this chance."

"Chance for what?" Erik asked.

"We're alone. You *know*. Nobody's here. Get it?" Jeremy hinted. "And look what I brought." He unzipped his backpack and pulled the bottle out of the pouch.

"What *is* that? It looks nasty."

"Let's see. Jaegermeister. I'm not really sure what it is," Jeremy admitted. "But it tastes okay. Try some."

"I'll pass."

"Come on. Try it for me," Jeremy coaxed. He swished the brownish liquid around in the bottle for effect.

"No thanks. I don't drink," Erik responded. "I didn't know you drank, either."

"I don't that often. Only when my life sucks." Jeremy opened the bottle and took a swallow. "Which is pretty much all of the time nowadays."

"Put it away, Jeremy. My mother's going to smell it on your breath."

Jeremy swigged a few more gulps and replied, "You're such a worrier. I've got breath mints in my bag."

"Please?" Erik said. He moved close to Jeremy and kissed him as he took the bottle out of his hand.

Without much convincing, Jeremy surrendered to Erik's kisses. Within minutes, they were laying down on the blanket with little space between them. Overheated in spite of the cooling night, piece by piece of clothing was shed until Erik realized that they were nearly naked. "Wait a sec," he panted.

"Come on Erik, don't freak out. I love you. I want you. I need you."

"Just take your time. I want to feel you here with me."

"I know what'll help you relax." He slid his hand down Erik's stomach and traveled south.

Erik scooted closer and closed his eyes as Jeremy resumed his previous wanderings. He let go of all the thoughts crowding his mind and yielded to Jeremy's caresses. Lost in the throes of lust, Erik didn't hear his mother calling his name throughout the house.

Trembling and aching from the release of sexual tension, he rolled over on the blanket and faced his lover. "Wow," was all he could say.

"I told you you'd like it," Jeremy said.

"I don't think I can move. What did you do to me?"

"You want me to do it again?"

"Oh my God. I think I'd die," Erik groaned. "But it'd definitely be a happy death."

"Then I guess we better wait until later tonight," Jeremy replied.

"I love you. I'm so glad you're here."

"Not as much as I am." Jeremy laid his head against Erik's taut stomach.

Just then, Erik heard his mother's voice clearly this time. "Erik, where are you two?"

"Oh crap," Erik said, bumping Jeremy off as he sat up. He grabbed his clothes and pulled them onto his shaking body. "Get dressed!" he hissed.

Erik yelled, "We're up here. In the tree house."

Marie opened the screen door and peered through the darkness. "Didn't you hear me calling you? What are you doing up there?"

"Just talking. We got bored with the computer."

"Well, I made some dessert, so come on down now."

"Be there in a sec," Erik answered and heard the screen door slam shut. "Oh man, I hope she doesn't suspect anything strange."

"Don't stress out. How could she know?"

"Just hurry up." Erik scaled down the ladder and waited for Jeremy at the bottom.

After a tense dessert, Erik helped his mother do the dishes. When he returned to his bedroom, Jeremy was under his covers. Erik saw a pile of clothes folded on the floor. "Come here," Jeremy said.

Erik didn't move. "Jeremy. My mom's still up. We can't get away with this." A disappointed look crossed his boyfriend's face and Erik almost capitulated. But he knew it would be crazy to risk it.

"Please...?"

"No way. Wait 'til she's asleep at least. I'm going to go sleep in the guest room since you're already in bed. I'll come to you later on," Erik promised. He gathered his things and settled himself in the other end of the house.

Erik sat on the bed thinking about what had just happened in the tree house. He had never been touched like that before and didn't quite know how to feel about it. His body desired more, while the synapses in his brain fired from apprehension to excitement and back again. "What am I supposed to want? What am I supposed to do?" he asked himself.

Lying in an unfamiliar bed and thinking about Jeremy lying in his own, resulted in little sleep. Erik rose at midnight and crept down the hallway to his bedroom. When he opened the door, it appeared that Jeremy was sleeping. But when he took a closer look, he realized that Jeremy was actually curled up in fetal position, rocking back and forth.

"Jeremy, what's wrong?" Erik rushed over and kneeled by the side of the bed. When Jeremy focused through his tears and recognized Erik's voice in the dark, he wrapped his arms around his neck and clung to him. Being so close, Erik could smell the alcohol on Jeremy's breath. Shifting his position to better hold up Jeremy's weight, Erik kicked an empty bottle across the floor. It clanked against the mirrored closet door and stopped. "You finished that whole thing?" he asked.

"You don't understand," Jeremy slurred. "I needed to. My life is shot to hell."

"That's not true. Can't you think of anything to be happy about?"

Jeremy grabbed the back of Erik's head and forced his tongue into his mouth for an answer. Erik drew back a little, but Jeremy pulled him down into bed with him. Erik could feel every inch of Jeremy's nakedness under his own pajamas. He breathed sharply and felt his body harden. Jeremy found Erik's hand and whispered, "Touch me—like I did to you."

"I want to. But not now. You're too drunk."

"Go on, take advantage of me. I want you to."

"When you sober up, I'd be happy to." Erik lifted himself off of Jeremy's body.

Jeremy yanked Erik back down. The motion of Jeremy's body rubbing against his conflicted Erik. It felt so good that he could barely make a decision. His nerve endings pulsated in remembrance of what Jeremy had done to him just hours ago. He felt Jeremy's lips suck at his chest and weave their way down his stomach again.

Erik shifted onto his side and pulled Jeremy's head back up to his. Their bodies glued together, Erik felt like he was suffocating. When he tried to get some space between them, Jeremy clung closer. Breathing hot, alcohol-tainted breath on Erik's face, Jeremy thrust against him.

"Jeremy, this isn't the way I want it to be."

"You can't always get what you want. But that's life."

"No, we need to stop. This isn't fun. It feels sick." Erik tried to twist away.

"Get over yourself, Erik. I'm tired of your morals and judgments—what are you, a saint?"

"What are you talking about?"

"No drinking. No sex. No fun."

"Why are you acting this way?"

"I'm just sick of waiting for everything to be okay. I just have to make it okay myself."

Erik sat up onto the edge of the bed and said, "You know what? It's stupid to discuss this right now. Let's talk in the morning, okay?"

"What? You're just going to leave me here alone?"

"I'll sit here with you until you fall asleep, but that's it. You aren't in your right state of mind. There'll be other times for sex."

"You promise?" Jeremy asked. "I want you so bad."

"I swear," Erik said, trying to calm his own body down.

In spite of his still aroused state, Jeremy yawned. "Did I ruin it?"

"No. You didn't ruin anything. Just stay sober next time, okay?"

Jeremy mumbled what sounded like an agreement and then passed out. Erik held him until he heard soft snores and then returned to the guest bedroom. All night he tossed and turned, replaying the night's events in his head.

The morning light slinking through the window woke Erik before anyone else. He snuck through his room so as to not disturb Jeremy and got into the shower. As soon as the water was on, however, Jeremy stirred and woke up groggy. He felt around the bed for another body but the sheets next to him remained cold.

As Erik toweled dry in the bathroom, he heard Jeremy clear his throat. He slid open the door and popped his wet head into the room. "Good morning."

"Not as good as it could have been," Jeremy grumbled.

Erik's smile dissolved. "I see you're still not feeling well. Can I get you some aspirin?"

Jeremy shook his head no, then yes, as the hangover throbbed in his forehead. "I needed you last night. And you didn't come through for me."

"Do you even remember what happened? You were pretty wasted."

"I remember you coming in, but then you refused to do anything with me."

"Only because you were drunk. Believe me; it was hard for me, too. I wanted you so much, but not enough to sleep

with someone who could barely put togeth
That's not the way I want it to be with you."

Jeremy turned over without answering
a bath towel around his waist and stepped
He sat down next to Jeremy's legs and said, _
sorry. Do you understand my dilemma?"

Jeremy hid his face. Erik reached over and began to
rub his back. "What can I do?"

Between sniffles, Jeremy finally responded. "I just
want you to love me. For someone to love me."

"I do. I do. I do," Erik pledged. "You're not worried
that I don't?"

"I just feel you pulling away from me. I don't think it's
just my imagination?"

"I want to be honest with you, Jeremy. But I'm afraid
of losing you."

Jeremy rolled onto his side toward Erik. "What? Just
say it."

"It just seems like I barely know you. I don't get the
drinking thing and sometimes you are really gentle and
other times so rough that it scares me. I feel like I never
know what to expect."

The tears began to fall, but Jeremy's face remained
stony. "It's over then?"

"You're not listening to me," Erik said. "I love you and
want to be with you; I'm just trying to tell you that I'm
concerned about you. You're so depressed and nothing
makes you happy anymore."

"*You* do."

"It's not healthy for me to be the only thing you like
about your life. I think you need some professional help.
Isabelle has an awesome therapist—I can get her number
for you," Erik offered.

Jeremy grabbed his pile of clothes and dressed without continuing the conversation. Erik waited until Jeremy was almost finished tying his shoes before speaking again. "Don't be upset. I'm not breaking up with you." He reached over and Jeremy's hand swatted him away.

"You know what, Erik? Actions speak louder than words." Jeremy kicked the bedpost.

"What's that supposed to mean?"

"It means that it's obvious that you don't want to be in a relationship with me. Clearly, I want more than you want. If you don't have the balls to be with me, then it's not going to work." Jeremy squatted next to his backpack and shoved his remaining belongings back into the large compartment. As he hoisted the bag onto his shoulder, a notebook dropped out of an unzipped pocket and skidded under Erik's bed.

Before he got to the bedroom door, Jeremy turned around and said, "Is it that guy who was watching you Friday night?"

"What in the world are you talking about?" Erik was beginning to wonder if Jeremy was still drunk.

"Don't act like you don't know. The guy at the race. He never took his eyes off of you the whole time," Jeremy accused. "I can tell something's going on."

"Come over here. Let's sit down and talk this out. There is no other guy. You're the only one I want."

"Well, you have a back-up now, 'cuz I'm gone!"

Erik begged him all the way down the hallway to come back and work things out, but Jeremy's mind was made up. Slamming the front door behind him, Jeremy broke into a run as soon as he hit the street. Erik stood in shock, deciding whether or not to chase after him. He dropped to the front steps, still wearing only a towel. "But I love *you*," he said to the empty street.

Chapter Fifteen

After getting dressed, Erik called down the hallway to his mother's room: "Bye Ma, we'll be back later this afternoon." He pretended that Jeremy was still with him and even spoke aloud to his imaginary friend as evidence. Although he didn't really feel like going without Jeremy, he walked down the street to Isabelle's house anyway. He got there just as Maxine's mother was dropping them off.

Erik greeted the girls and tried to act like nothing was wrong. But Isabelle could tell. "Hey, where's Jeremy?"

"Thanks again for helping out with the race," Erik said. "Did you two have fun last night?"

"Wait a minute. You didn't answer me. Where did Jeremy go?"

Erik wavered on a lie. "Promise not to tell? We had a disagreement this morning and he took off. I don't know where he went."

Isabelle frowned. "Should we go look for him?"

"I have no idea where he went. I was standing there on my porch wearing only a towel—I couldn't exactly run after him butt-naked."

"What did you two fight about?" Maxine asked.

Erik turned red and answered, "Uh, we just don't see eye to eye about what we want our relationship to be. I didn't think we'd break up over it, but—"

"You guys actually broke up!" Isabelle shouted.

"Shh! I don't know if we broke up or not. I didn't think it was that big of a deal, but before we could work it out, he just ran off."

"Maybe he just needs to think things over and he'll come back later today," Maxine said.

"I guess all we can do is wait," Isabelle agreed.

Erik had more than an uneasy feeling about not going out and immediately looking for his boyfriend, but he convinced himself that Jeremy just needed some time alone to figure things out and then he'd be back.

For a few more minutes, they stood on the porch debating whether or not to go to church or look for Jeremy when Joshua pulled up. As they climbed into the Subaru and drove towards Lake Park, Erik fibbed about why Jeremy wasn't with them. Covertly, the three of them sat in the backseat scoping the landscape for signs of Jeremy.

Nearing the church, Isabelle found her palms sweating. Sensing her anxiety, Maxine reached over and held Isabelle's hand. "Don't worry," she whispered. "Remember what Reverend Kat said."

Isabelle looked at the groups of people gathering in the parking lot. There were women with shaved heads and men with ponytails and women with ponytails and men with shaved heads. There were singles, couples, and families. Some were wearing suits and dresses, others shorts and flip-flops. Regardless of attire, the crowd seemed pleasant enough to Isabelle.

They spilled out of the wagon, Maxine still holding Isabelle's hand. Isabelle's instinct was to let go once they were in 'public' but soon realized that many of the couples were also holding hands.

Erik was just as nervous as Isabelle and only relaxed once they were inside. The five of them sat in a middle set of pews and waited for the service to begin. For Isabelle, it was a people-watching festival. She couldn't stop staring at the hundred or so gay people filling up the sanctuary. Erik, however, focused inwardly. He kept thinking about Jeremy and closed his eyes until the call to worship.

Stepping in front of the pulpit, a woman with medium-length blonde hair said, "Welcome, everyone. Do we have any first-time visitors here?" Maxine, sitting in-between Erik and Isabelle, nudged each of them with an elbow, prompting them to raise their hands with her.

The woman's eyes settled on them. "You're in the right place," she said. Isabelle remembered that voice and could now see the deep dimples she'd heard over the phone last night when Reverend Kat had laughed.

Isabelle found herself smiling back for the rest of the service, keeping her eyes planted on the pastor. When the band got up to play, Isabelle soon realized that she was not in a Catholic church. She found her feet tapping and hands clapping as they sang praise and worship songs before the sermon began.

Erik sat still. He wished that Jeremy was sitting beside him. "We'll get over it," he consoled himself. "He'll come with us next Sunday."

During Reverend Kat's sermon, Isabelle listened critically, waiting for the pastor to say something that she could refute or dismiss. What she waited for, she never heard. Even if she didn't understand all the God-talk, as she dubbed it, Isabelle's skepticism faded as the message concluded. "Not bad," she said to Maxine. "She's got some interesting ideas."

Reverend Tony, who had been sitting at the piano for most of the service, announced, "Donuts and coffee in the Rec Hall! We want all of our first-time visitors to come introduce themselves to us."

"Are we staying?" Isabelle asked Joshua and Matthew.

"Sure, if you want to. We usually socialize for a little while before going back to work," Matthew said.

Joshua and Matthew led them into the social hall, and they felt all eyes on them as they made their way to where Reverend Kat and Tony were greeting people. "Why is everyone looking at us?" Isabelle whispered to Joshua.

"It's just because you're new."

"It's kind of scary," she said. "I feel like I'm in some kind of fishbowl."

"It gets easier. Everyone has to get past the 'being new' stage. Eventually, you'll feel right at home here," he assured her.

Maxine got past that stage within seconds. She'd made eye contact with a group of twenty-something people lounging on some couches, and they beckoned her over. Maxine tried to pull Isabelle with her, but Isabelle dropped her hand.

She was fixated on Reverend Kat. Something in this person drew her in, something that Isabelle hadn't felt before. It felt deceptively like a crush, but Isabelle knew it wasn't that. She just had to find out what made Rev. Kat glow from the inside out.

As soon as she stood in front of Reverend Kat, Isabelle was dumbstruck. She rocked back and forth with her lips parted, waiting for words to arise, but none came.

"Are you the one I talked to on the phone last night?" Kat helped her out. "I had a feeling you'd show up today."

"You did? How?"

"Oh, just a feeling."

"All I wanted to know was about the club."

"Then why are you here *today*?" If Reverend Kat hadn't been smiling and speaking in such a gentle voice, Isabelle would have been tempted to run out.

"My friends wanted to come. I didn't even decide until this morning."

Reverend Kat put her hand on Isabelle's arm and said, "Well, we're glad you did. Come again, y'hear?" Then she turned to Matthew and Joshua, asking them if they had gotten in the book that she'd ordered last week.

Isabelle saw Erik and Maxine sitting on the couches with six or seven other people. She made her way over, avoiding eye contact with everyone she passed until she was in front of Maxine.

"Sit down, Izzy," she said, pulling Isabelle into her lap.

One of the girls next to them said, "You two are such a cute couple. Aren't they?"

"I'm Isabelle," she introduced herself.

"Oh we know all about you," one young woman said. "You've got some real fans here."

Maxine laughed. "I guess you could call us that."

"Are any of you going to the youth meeting on the 27th?" Maxine asked.

"Well, technically we're not allowed because we're too old, dang it," a guy with a goatee said. "We never had any gay clubs when I was in high school."

"I know. You guys are so lucky," another girl added.

"We're pretty excited about it," Maxine said.

Isabelle lifted herself off Maxine's lap. "Joshua and Matthew are waiting, so we better get going."

"It was nice meeting you; hope you come again," Goatee man said.

"I have a feeling we'll be back," Maxine answered for the three of them.

As they were leaving the social hall, Isabelle turned around one last time to catch a glimpse of Reverend Kat. She saw the pastor talking with a tall, thin woman who had been leading the band that morning. They were standing in a way that indicated their relationship was beyond casual. "That must be her partner," Isabelle decided. Just then, Rev. Kat looked her way and tapped her friend. The tall woman smiled and waved at Isabelle and then the two of them went back to their conversation.

"Am I really so self-centered to think that they're talking about me?" Isabelle mused on the way to the parking lot.

Joshua popped in a CD and Erik asked, "Why does this music sound familiar?"

"It's a CD the church band made last year during our annual conference," Matthew answered.

"Can we get copies of it?" Maxine wanted to know.

"Sure. They sell them at the church. I think we even have a few left at the store. You guys mind if we go by there? I was going to drop Joshua off for work and then take you all home."

"No problem! I've been wanting to see the store," Isabelle said.

Erik murmured in agreement, though his mind was still preoccupied by Jeremy. "God, is he okay?" he asked as he immersed himself in the music filling the car.

Chapter Sixteen

If only Erik had asked that question a few hours earlier. While they'd been on their way to church, Jeremy had returned to the bridge by himself. This time it was broad daylight and he had to be careful so as not to be seen, and especially not to be stopped. What had been a spontaneous decision the first time was now a calculated one. All the way to the bridge, Jeremy plotted. There wasn't much to plot really—just some things to go over in his mind to prepare himself.

This time as he hung onto a cable above the road and river, his mind was resolute. He wasn't nervous. He had no second thoughts. His hand released the thick wire and he propelled his body forward into the air. All he proclaimed before plunging spread eagle into the rushing water was, "I'm sorry."

Later that afternoon, Matthew dropped the kids off at the Foxfire house and Jeremy was still nowhere to be found. "I have a sick feeling about this," Erik said. "I think he might be in danger."

The girls couldn't disagree. "What do you think we should do?" Maxine asked.

"Maybe we should tell my parents," Isabelle said.

"No, not yet. Let me make a few phone calls first," Erik said. He scanned his memory bank for Adam's phone number and, after three attempts, reached Jeremy's best friend. A brief conversation let him know that Adam hadn't seen Jeremy since the day he ran away from home. Erik called Joshua at the store and told him what happened.

After Erik finished, Joshua implored, "You need to call the police. It's going to be dark soon and it's just not safe for him to be out wandering around. We'll keep our eyes open over here."

"That's what I was afraid you would say. But I guess you're right." Hanging up the phone, Erik said, "Let's go talk to your Mom, Isabelle."

Ana was in the kitchen preparing dinner when the downcast trio graced the doorway. "What's wrong?"

"It's Jeremy. He's gone," Erik sputtered.

"Gone? No one knows where he went?"

"Erik and he got in an argument this morning and Jeremy ran off," Isabelle explained. Erik covered his eyes with his hands.

"He's been gone since before you left this morning?"

"Sorry we lied to you," Maxine said. "But we thought he'd be back by now."

"This is serious. Jeremy's in trouble. Emotionally, if not physically." Ana picked up the phone and called Jeremy's parents. "He didn't come home?" she repeated to Jeremy's father on the other line. They could all hear his reaction to the news that Jeremy was missing. Ana held the phone out from her ear while Jeremy's father lambasted her for not supervising his son. "Listen Steve. We need to work together. He ran away from you. He ran away from us. It's the same issue—Jeremy needs help and it's our job to provide it for him. I'm calling the police." Ana hung up.

She unhunched her shoulders and took a deep breath before dialing 9-1-1. After answering a series of questions, the dispatcher told her that they would send a squad car over to the house to get some more information. "Technically, we don't usually send out a search party until the person has been missing for 24 hours, but since you said the boy originally ran away a few days ago, he may be in greater trouble."

Ana sat down at the kitchen table and beckoned the kids to join her. "You should have said something earlier, but it's still not your fault that he ran away. Jeremy was on the edge. Even I didn't realize how close."

For the next fifteen minutes, they sat in silence, each contemplating how he or she could have stopped Jeremy from running away. A knock on the door snapped their heads to attention, each of them hoping that Jeremy would be on the other side. The four of them crowded around the door as Ana opened it. Two uniformed officers waited with clipboards in hand. "May we come in?"

They backed into the kitchen and allowed the police to interrogate them. After asking all of the standard missing persons questions, the officers were just about to ask for some items of Jeremy's clothing to help the rescue dogs find him, when a frantic ringing of the doorbell took place. Ana rushed back down the hallway and opened it to find a harried couple standing on the porch. "Is he back? Have you heard anything?" Jeremy's mother pushed into the Foxfire house.

"Come in, Mrs. Hayes," Ana said, knowing that they were way past the point of introductions. "The police are here. Maybe you can fill in some of the details."

When the couple entered the kitchen, Jeremy's mother cried, "My baby! Why aren't you out looking for him?"

"Calm down, Jessica," her husband said, surveying the inhabitants of the room. His eyes settled on Erik's tear-stained face. Piece by piece, the puzzle fell into place. "It's you," Mr. Hayes charged. "Goddamn it. You're the one who caused all of this." He pointed at Erik and all eyes in the room fell on him.

Erik scooted his chair back. Jeremy's father growled, "Tell us where he is!"

The female police officer, Stanley, her badge read, stepped between the two. "Sir, I'm going to ask you to step back. You're not helping."

Steve held his hands up and said, "Hey, I'm just telling you guys what happened. This kid here..."

Officer Stanley cut him off. "Excuse me, but making accusations will not bring your son back. Please sit down and tell us the facts about the night Jeremy left."

Leaving out many pertinent details, especially regarding their reaction to their son telling them he was gay, the couple recounted their last evening with their son.

"We'll call you as soon as we know anything. I suggest you use this time to support each other and not lay blame," Officer Stanley suggested, before shutting the door.

The adults watched the hours tick by on the kitchen clock, waiting for the police to call, while the kids stayed in Isabelle's room, trying to solve the mystery themselves.

As soon as they were behind closed doors, Erik burst out, "I know it's all my fault! If only I hadn't started that fight this morning!"

"Stop Erik. You're gonna make yourself sick. Come here, honey." Isabelle cradled her friend. "Shh...shh..." she whispered, stroking his hair.

Maxine sat on the edge of the bed. "Let's brainstorm all of the places we think he might have gone."

Erik sniffled and choked on his tears. "I don't think they're going to find him. He's just gone."

Isabelle pushed Erik up and held him at arm's length. "What do you mean? Erik, is there something you haven't told us?"

"I don't know. He's just been so depressed lately. I've been worried about him before, but not like this. I didn't realize how serious it was," he answered. "And last night he was drinking a lot."

"Did he ever say anything about wanting to commit...?" Maxine asked.

"Don't say it!" Isabelle clapped her hand over Maxine's mouth. "Don't even think it."

"Sorry," Maxine's muffled voice said.

"I know. We just can't give up hope," Isabelle said.

When the doorbell rang a few hours later, everyone in the house snapped out of the lull of waiting and ran helter-skelter to the door. Ana fumbled with the lock and swung the door open. Officer Stanley held up a battered-looking backpack and asked, "Does this look familiar?" For a moment, no one made a sound. Then Jessica's gentle weeping turned into a howl. The officers led the families into the living room and sat everyone down.

"We found it on the bridge," the other officer, Mack, said. He opened the bag and dumped the contents out on the coffee table. Jeremy's clothes fell out and the empty liquor bottle with them. "That's just one clue," he said. "We can only assume that he'd been drinking. There are a few other clues, but nothing overwhelmingly significant. Unless you folks can shed some light on anything you see here."

Erik's stomach almost turned when he saw the bottle. He hoped that no one could see the green coloring his face. Officer Stanley said, "Mack, I'm going to accompany Erik outside. He looks like he needs some air." Lifting him up by his arm, Stanley led Erik to the sliding glass door.

The cool air did settle Erik's nerves a little bit, but the presence of the uniformed officer standing so near him riled them back up again. "Am I in trouble?" Erik asked.

"Should you be?" She smiled at him.

"I don't know," he admitted.

"Well, usually when people ask that question, it's because they think or know that they've done something wrong," she explained. "Which is it?"

Erik took a deep breath. "I can't believe how out of control this has gotten."

"You want to start from the beginning? You know, I came into this thing pretty late in the game."

Shifting his weight back and forth, Erik looked like he might fall over. "Why don't you sit down here next to me?" Officer Stanley invited. "I won't bite, I swear."

"I can't tell you anything. I want to, but I can't."

"How 'bout I ask you some questions and you can decide if you want to answer them."

Erik didn't move.

"Tell me about Jeremy. Just anything you want to about him," she suggested.

"Well, he's about my height and weight. But his hair's darker..." Erik started.

She cleared her throat. "No, I mean about his personality. You two are good friends, right? You might be able to tell me something that leads us to him."

"Um, well. He's really funny and very passionate about things. And smart. He's read just about every classic there is. He's outgoing and is always looking for new adventures." Erik's eyes grew bright as he talked. "Jeremy's unpredictable, though. Sometimes he gets depressed and not much cheers him up."

"Was this morning one of those days?" she asked.

Erik nodded. "He left my house in a dark mood. I thought it would pass, though. I've seen it before and he always snaps out of it."

Officer Stanley asked, "Did something happen when he was at your house this morning that triggered him to run off?"

Erik didn't respond.

"Erik, it's not your fault that he ran away." Her calm and unaccusing voice led Erik to trust her.

"But it is!" he declared. "I disappointed him. I ruined things. I wasn't there for him."

She put her hand on his arm and said, "Tell me."

Relinquishing the inhibition he'd been clinging to, Erik told her about their secret relationship and the pressures Jeremy and he faced at home. "I can't believe I'm telling you this," he punctuated his monologue with every few sentences. But the more he told her, the more he wanted to tell her.

Officer Stanley jotted some notes down on her pad. When Erik was finished with his story, she asked, "Is it possible that he left anything at your house that might help us out?"

"Like what?" Erik asked.

"Maybe a note or a book. Something that might indicate his state of mind. I'm just fishing for clues here."

"I haven't been home since he left. Maybe there's something. I can go look," he offered.

"Why don't we go over there together?"

Erik hesitated. "It's better if I go alone."

"I understand," she said. "I'll wait outside." The two of them walked up the block to Erik's house and Officer Stanley kept her word while Erik went inside.

He slipped into his room without alerting his mother. Everything looked just as it had when he'd left for church this morning. Erik halted in his tracks when he saw the unmade bed still showing the indentations of Jeremy's sleeping body. He lay down on the bed, his cheek against the pillowcase. Closing his eyes, he breathed in, savoring the smell of Jeremy's cologne still lingering on the material. Erik replayed the past twenty-four hours in his mind, hoping to recover a clue that would help find Jeremy. Nothing came.

Erik forced himself to open his eyes, but didn't move his head off of the pillow. From this sideways angle, he saw the closet door mirror reflecting something underneath the bed-frame. Reaching down with his left arm, he pulled the hard edge of the small notepad out into the light. He'd never seen it before, but knew that it must be Jeremy's. It was bound together with a black rubber band. Erik remembered hearing the slap of the cover hitting his hardwood floor before Jeremy had run out this morning.

Shoving it into his coat pocket, he snuck back out of the house and ran up to Officer Stanley. "I found something," he said, handing her the journal. "I don't know what's in it. I didn't look yet."

She got out her flashlight and thumbed through the pages. This miniature notebook—in its fragments and veiled references—told her the complete story. Most of it she skimmed through, but when she got to one particular page, bookmarked by the flyer for the GLBTQ youth group, she stopped.

"What is it?" Erik's words froze as he realized what she held in her hand.

Looking around the empty street, she handed Erik the open page. Erik read it, hearing every word from Jeremy's mouth as though he was standing there. He wanted to deny it, to destroy the evidence, to go back in time and not find it. Officer Stanley caught him just before he hit the ground. She laid him out on the lawn and swished a vial of smelling salts in front of his nose. Erik jerked up. "Oh my God!" he wailed over and over while the officer held him.

She lifted him up and said, "I think it's time to talk to your parents." Unable to resist, Erik allowed her to lead him back up his front steps. With one hand propping him up, the other rang the doorbell. Marie stood stunned as Officer Stanley told her what they had just discovered.

On the verge of collapse, the two women helped Erik into his bed and stood at the door whispering. Officer Stanley told Marie a little more of the story, omitting the true nature of Erik and Jeremy's relationship. "Keep an eye on him," she admonished. "Check his room every half-hour, okay?" Marie nodded and posted herself in a chair right outside her son's door for the remainder of the night.

When Officer Stanley arrived back at the Foxfire residence, the vigil in the living room was still going strong. All eyes landed on her as she walked into the room clutching the small, black notebook. She handed it to Officer Mack, with her finger marking the page she wanted him to read.

"Come with me," he beckoned Jeremy's parents into another room.

From the living room, all ears strained to hear his report. While they couldn't decipher the officer's words exactly, the reaction from Jeremy's parents filled them in. Loud sobs and angry voices cut through the air.

"Officer Stanley? Can you come in here, please?" Officer Mack called. Jeremy's mother's face was crimson and his father's knuckles were white from clenching. Neither one of them said anything when she walked in.

"This is only evidence," she said. "We don't have all of the answers, yet. Sometimes kids write things like this and don't follow through. We're going to do some more investigating tonight and will call as soon as we learn anything. Mack, can you escort them to their car?" At first they resisted, but then conceded to the officers' promptings. The couple stumbled to their car and sat in silence before turning the ignition and driving home.

Back in the Foxfire living room, Officer Stanley explained, "We have a job to finish now. We'll be sure to notify you when we get more information." They all nodded, still curious as to what the black notebook held and why Erik hadn't returned with her.

Chapter Seventeen

It wasn't until five o'clock the next evening that the awaited phone calls came. Officer Stanley dialed number after number—first to Jeremy's parents, next to Erik, then to the Foxfires—each message bearing the same news: "The search crew found him...washed up on the river's edge...looks like he jumped off the bridge...sorry for your loss...let us know if you need support services..."

Erik didn't get out of bed for the next three days. There he lay mute, sick, and immobile. On the third day his mother called on Isabelle for help. "I can't do it alone," she admitted. "I know I told you to not come over here, but I think he'll listen to you."

"I'll be right over," Isabelle replied, instantly forgiving Mrs. Pennington for keeping her away.

As soon as she dropped the phone back in its cradle, Isabelle ran up the street to Erik's house and let herself in the front door. "I'm here," she yelled to Mrs. Pennington and jogged down the hallway to Erik's room. She knocked, but didn't wait for a response. Upon entering the room, she was struck by the heaviness in the air.

"Boy, you need some oxygen," she declared, twisting the blinds and sliding open the window. "No wonder you're sick!" Erik squinted and pulled the covers over his eyes to shield them from the unfamiliar light.

Isabelle sat down and put her hand on his clammy skin. "Erik. Talk to me. Your mother said you haven't said a word in three days."

His eyes teared up as he shook his head. Isabelle reached over to his nightstand and put a tissue in his hand. "Come on, Erik. You have to snap out of this."

"Snap out of it? What the hell do you know?"

Isabelle changed her tactic midstream. "I'm sorry, honey. That was insensitive of me. I just want to help you."

"No one helped Jeremy. Why do I deserve someone to help me?" Erik muttered.

"I know you're hurting. And I know that nothing I say is going to make it all better, but I don't want you to *die* over it," Isabelle pleaded. "You're wasting away in here."

"I just don't care anymore, Isabelle. You don't understand how this feels."

"You're right, I don't. But remember when I tried to die over Mandy breaking up with me last year? You were worried and wanted to make things better, right?"

"Yeah, but that's different. Jeremy's really dead and it's all my fault."

"Erik, Jeremy *is* dead. And it's not your fault. It's everyone's fault. And no one in particular's fault."

"What are you talking about?"

"We all helped kill him, in a way," she began. "If this stupid society wasn't so homophobic, his parents wouldn't have rejected him, you wouldn't have been so fearful of being "caught" being in love with him, people at school wouldn't have beaten up on him, the list goes on. It may

116

seem like a cop-out excuse, but I've been thinking about it a lot."

Erik raised his head off the pillow and propped himself up. "You can't just blame it on society. There are lots of gay people who don't end up jumping off bridges."

"True. But, I wonder how many of us have considered it," she countered. "You know I have, many times. Haven't you? Hasn't there been a time when you just felt like you just couldn't face another hour of this life?"

Erik was quiet for a long time. He scanned his brain, stopping briefly on every moment that he'd slightly or seriously considered suicide. "I guess the thoughts have crossed my mind. But I never got to the point of even getting close to going through with it."

"But it helps you understand Jeremy's feelings better. Think back to the time when you most closely considered doing it. That's the place where Jeremy was a few days ago. But instead of turning back around, he kept going. That's the only difference between him and us. We always turn back around for some reason or another. He didn't."

Erik leaned back against the headboard. "I still just keep thinking that I could have stopped him, somehow."

"There is that possibility, but it doesn't do any good now. All that results in is you beating yourself up for next fifty years," Isabelle said.

"But what do I do then? I just can't let it be meaningless. I loved him, Isabelle. And I can't get it out of my mind. I keep picturing him falling, drowning, and what he must have looked like washing up on the shore. His beautiful face and body smashed and bloody..."

"Well, it's not going to go away *immediately*. But I think it would help for you to get out of bed and start living your life again."

"If I get up, I feel like I'm betraying him."

"If you *don't* get up, you will be."

"What do you mean?"

"Well, what good are you doing for Jeremy's memory if you stay here wasting away?" Isabelle asked. "The funeral's tomorrow—Friday, if you've lost track of the days. Have you thought about going?"

"I don't see how I can. Mr. Hayes will probably send me to my own grave."

"Jeremy's father won't bother you. Plus, it doesn't matter what he thinks. It's more important that you be there for Jeremy's sake. At least then he'll know how much you cared."

"I have to think about it."

"There's nothing to think about. The worst has already happened. All we can do now is not let this happen to anyone else we know," Isabelle declared.

"How can *we* prevent other people from killing themselves if we couldn't help Jeremy?"

Isabelle thought for a minute before answering. "Well, I guess we just have to work on changing society, then."

Erik almost laughed. "Change society? Yeah right."

"I'm serious, Erik. It's been done before—look at the Civil Rights movement. Give me some time to think about it." Isabelle moved towards the door. "Now, as for you, young man. I want you to get up out of that deathbed and into the shower. You stink." She waggled her finger at him from the doorway.

Erik felt his mood lift a little. "I guess I can do that. What then?"

"Well, come over to my house, of course. My family's been asking about you every day."

"Alright. See you later, Izzy," Erik said. "And thanks..."

"Hey, you've done the same for me many times over," she said, shutting the door behind her. Mrs. Pennington had been lingering in the hallway eavesdropping on the latter part of their conversation. Isabelle simply said, "Don't worry about Erik. He's gonna be okay now." The sound of the shower confirmed her pronouncement.

As Isabelle walked down the block, she began to think about what she'd proposed to Erik. Tuesday, the day after Jeremy's body had been recovered, the principal of Lakepark High had called Principal Martinez from Foresthill with the news of Jeremy's death. Isabelle had been sitting in her first period class when the principal's voice came over the scratchy intercom. He announced that a student from Lakepark had committed suicide and encouraged Foresthill students to show their support by attending the memorial service on Friday. Her classmates murmured rumors and speculations and Isabelle wondered how supportive they would be if they found out that Jeremy was gay.

Kicking a bottle cap into the gutter Isabelle said aloud, "I'm sick of the secrecy. If we just pretend that this was a suicide for no apparent reason, then it's meaningless." She walked up her front path and sat down on the steps. There she remained in contemplation until she saw Erik's figure appear on the horizon.

His stooped shoulders and drooping head, arms sewn tightly to his ribcage, were the mark of a much older, broken man. "If I don't think of something, I'm gonna lose him, too," she thought. Erik glanced around the street and then refocused his eyes on each square of pavement that was the sidewalk leading to Isabelle's house.

When he was little Erik often counted how many squares it took to get to his best friend's house. This afternoon he didn't start counting until he had already walked half a block from his doorstep. "One-hundred and forty-six," he announced when he arrived.

"I thought it was two-hundred and thirteen."

"Yeah, it is," Erik said. "I started late."

"I was watching you. Could tell that you were counting your steps."

"I don't know what provoked me. I just remembered being a kid for a few minutes there."

"Not a bad thing."

"Sometimes I just wish I could go back. Be innocent and unaware."

"I know what you mean. But, hey, let's not get depressed about it. We've got work to do."

Erik followed Isabelle into the house and, after greeting her parents and assuring them that he was okay, they sequestered themselves in Isabelle's bedroom. "Do you mind if I call Max over?"

Erik handed her the phone. "What's been going on with you two since, um, I haven't been around."

Isabelle dialed the number and pursed her lips to shush Erik's question while she asked for Maxine. With some negotiating of transportation and timing, Maxine would be soon on her way.

"Now I'll tell you," Isabelle said, as she hung up the phone. "Let me rewind. The night we found out about Jeremy she stayed over here with me. Nothing happened between us, of course. We were so focused on the tragedy." Isabelle scratched her head with the edge of a comb. "To tell you the truth, not much has happened anyway. We've kissed a couple of times, but not much more. Not that I don't want to rip her clothes off every time I see her."

Erik started to laugh but felt his chest constrict. Fighting to catch his breath, he said, "I keep feeling like I'm suffocating. Like I can't get enough air into my lungs sometimes." He clamped his hand over his heart to keep it from exploding through his skin.

"Probably a panic attack," Isabelle diagnosed. "I used to get those when I got really stressed out. Lay down on the floor. I'll take you through a guided relaxation."

Erik scrunched his face up.

"I said, get down on the floor." Isabelle kicked one of his feet out from under him.

Once flat on his back, Erik tried to protest. "No offense, but is this one of your mother's hippie remedies?"

"No, silly. I learned it from my therapist. Haven't you noticed how much calmer I am since I've been seeing her?"

"Go ahead. Let's get this over with."

Isabelle led Erik through some deep breathing exercises to loosen his chest and then began to speak in a soothing voice. In the midst of the mythic journey Isabelle was weaving about waterfalls and the swishing of trees in a deep, dark forest, Maxine stood outside the door covering her mouth.

Maxine's giggles eventually burst through her fingers and she heard silence from behind the door. She cracked it open and peeked in at Isabelle frozen over Erik's feet.

"Am I interrupting something?" Maxine asked, with a straight face.

All three burst into laughter. "No respect," Isabelle said, shaking her head. "Come here, you."

Maxine leaned into Isabelle's arms and purred, "Mmm...mmm...."

"I'll take that as you're happy to see me?"

"That's an understatement!"

Forgetting that Erik was still lying on the floor between them, they held hands and gazed into each other's eyes. Erik coughed and said, "Um, this is a little awkward. Mind if I get up?"

The girls split apart, each one grabbing one of Erik's arms and pulled him up. "Sorry about that," Maxine said, hugging him. "It's just that Isabelle has this affect on me. How do you handle being around her?"

"I truly do not know."

"Whatcha got cookin' Isabelle?" Maxine asked. "I recognized that 'I've got a plan' voice over the phone."

"Very perceptive. I'm finally ready to unveil my idea."

Erik raised his eyebrows. "Hey, I thought we made a pact to not make any more pacts this year."

"That was last week," Isabelle said. "Silly rabbit."

Erik groaned and covered his face. "Count me out."

"You don't even know what I'm going to say!"

"I don't have the energy for anything right now."

"Hear me out, at least."

Maxine said, "Of course, we'll hear you out." She patted Erik on the head.

"Mr. Kinney gave us this assignment," she began. "To write a scene and stage it. I've written the scene already, but I was thinking about putting together like a public service announcement. You know, like those thirty second ads on TV."

"Like those old 'this is your brain on drugs' commercials?" Maxine asked.

"Exactly. But not exactly. I thought we could make one about tolerance and acceptance of peoples' differences and air it at school."

"We?" Erik asked.

"Yeah, we all could act in it," Isabelle said.

"That sounds like a blast. Is it that script you read to me?" Maxine asked.

"No, it's a new one," Isabelle answered.

As Erik listened, he imagined his classmates cracking jokes as they watched the video or even worse, targeting those who appeared in it. He said, "No thanks."

The girls' chatter dissolved. "What do you mean?"

"Let me explain and don't get pissed, Izzy," Erik stated. "I just can't imagine subjecting myself to more hell. I think I'm going to fade into the background and let things cool off. I'm just going to return to being Erik Pennington, the guy who everyone recognizes but doesn't really know. See you guys later." Before they could protest, he picked up his bag and walked to the door. Turning back he said, "I thought I could do it, but I can't."

"Don't leave, Erik. Come on. We'll drop the subject. We can hang out and have fun," Isabelle pleaded.

"Nah. I don't want to ruin things for you. See ya." He slipped out the door.

Isabelle jumped up to stop him, but Maxine pulled her back. "Let him go, Isabelle. He's still mourning. All we can do is be there for him when he's ready."

Isabelle struggled against Maxine's hand on her arm for a moment before relenting. "Maybe you're right," she conceded. "But I just want my old Erik back."

Chapter Eighteen

Erik almost hit his mother with the door, but barely noticed that she was standing there when he ran head first into his father's chest. Erik jerked backwards as if shocked by an electric fence. "Dad?" he said. "You're home?"

Jack Sr. looked trim and fit in his military garb, though his weary eyes betrayed his upright composure. "I'm home," he confirmed. "You take good care of your mother while I was gone?"

Erik stood a little taller and tucked his shirt. He wished that he would've been prepared for this moment, but it was almost as if he'd forgotten he had a father. In fact, he'd almost decided that he was better off without one. The pinkness of guilt rose in his cheeks and Erik glanced at his mother who nodded her head before he responded. "Yes, we did just fine."

"Who's going to get me something cold to drink?" Jack asked. The suitcases sitting in the foyer indicated that he'd been home only minutes before Erik opened the door. Jack escorted Erik into the house, while Marie retrieved him a beer from the fridge.

"How are you, Dad? Are you back for good now? What was it like?" Erik filled the silence with questions.

"Let's take a seat in the family room. I'm beat," Jack stated. They sat down on opposite ends of the couch and stared at each other's stranger-ness. "Looks like you've grown. I know it's only been a couple of weeks, but it seems like a lifetime."

"I think I *have* grown," Erik said.

"You've grown and I've just aged." He laughed in a gravelly voice.

Gauging the conversation as benign, Erik let himself relax into the couch. "We're actually having a civil conversation," he thought. "Maybe war has changed him."

"Can you tell me anything about what you were doing while you were gone?" Erik asked.

"No—it's still classified. But you can tell me what *you* were doing while I was gone," Jack said.

Erik stiffened against the back of the couch and knew that he'd better answer quickly. "Well, I pulled off that charity run we were planning before you left."

"Leadership. That's what marks the Pennington men. I was wondering when it would kick in for you." He squeezed Erik's knee, causing him to wince. "You're probably starting to think about which branch you want to join, but remember that we're a Marines family."

When Jack let go, Erik continued on about the fundraiser. "I loved leading the group. It was awesome how they all listened to me and did what I told them to do. I can't wait to show you the pictures Isabelle took when she gets them developed."

Jack's lips turned down at Isabelle's name. "I keep telling you son, you need to meet other girls. How do you expect to get a girlfriend when everyone sees you with *her* all of the time?"

Biting back his usual "but she's my best friend" speech, Erik was about to change the subject when Marie entered and set the beer on a coaster before her husband. She helped him lean back and eased his shoes off. "Dinner'll be ready soon. Why don't you take a little nap?"

Jack took a sip and settled into the cushions. "I may just do that."

Erik stood up and said, "Well, I've got a lot of schoolwork to make up, so I'll be in my room if anyone needs me."

"Make-up work?" Jack sat up. "You haven't been missing school have you?"

"I was out a few days." Erik looked at his mother to see if she had revealed any information to her husband yet, but her eyes were focused on the beads of water gliding down the side of the beer bottle. "Did Mom tell you about my friend Jeremy?"

Jack shook his head. "That kid from Lake Park?"

Swallowing the lump in his throat, Erik said, "Yeah. The guy I hung out with over the summer. Well, he killed himself earlier this week and the funeral's tomorrow."

His father's drooping eyes now stood at attention. "Committed suicide? Holy Christ! Why on earth would he do something like that?"

"His life was pretty messed up," Erik answered. "Apparently, he just couldn't handle it anymore so he jumped off the bridge."

"I'm sorry to hear about your friend," Jack said. "I liked him. He was a nice kid."

"Yeah, he was my best friend," Erik allowed himself to say. "I took a couple days off school to deal with it. I'm okay now, though."

Numbing the feelings rising up to contradict his words, Erik then excused himself to his bedroom. Once behind closed doors, tears streamed down his cheeks and he sobbed his way into his bathroom. "You're such a goddamn hypocrite," he said to his image in the mirror.

As for tomorrow's funeral, Erik still hadn't decided whether or not to show up. It seemed like making even the smallest decision overwhelmed him. Even though it was barely six o'clock, Erik crawled back into the cocoon of his bed and forced himself to fall asleep. He'd grown accustomed to hoping that when he woke, he'd find that it all had been a nightmare.

Two-hundred and thirteen squares of pavement down the street, the mood was charged with a different kind of tension as Maxine and Isabelle planned their evening. Though they'd spent the night together many times before as friends, they anticipated that tonight would be different.

After spending the evening playing board games with Kotamo family, Isabelle and Maxine headed out to the barn dragging sleeping bags behind them. With no lights, except for the kerosene lantern and the stars in the sky, the lightheartedness of their game playing faded. Isabelle spread the sleeping bag over a few bales of hay and zipped the other one to it.

Isabelle crawled into the makeshift bed and pulled the cover back for Maxine to join her. Maxine unhooked the lantern from the door and set it on a milking stool near the stable. Then she lay down next to Isabelle, avoiding skin contact as she crackled against the hay.

"I don't know how much longer I can stand this," she thought to herself.

"What?"

"Mmm. I didn't say anything," Maxine answered, rolling onto her side to face Isabelle.

"You were thinking so loud I could almost hear you. Not quite, though."

"It's nothing. Just random thoughts."

Isabelle stretched open her arms. "Why are you so far away? Come closer."

"Do you know what you're getting into?"

"Yes, and I want it."

"What is *it* that you want?"

"I want you."

"Are you sure?"

"Yes."

Isabelle drew Maxine towards her. Their lips inches apart, Isabelle said, "It's funny, but I'm not scared anymore."

"That's good, because now I am," Maxine replied.

"You don't need to be. I love you."

Maxine's heart pounded, rushing blood through every inch of her body. "You don't know how long I've wanted that to be true."

"I've been feeling it for a long time but wanted to make sure it was real before I said anything."

"I'm glad you waited. I practically told you that I loved you before I even met you, remember?"

"It's nice to hear it aloud, though." Isabelle planted her lips on Maxine's before she could reply.

Unlike the other kisses they shared, with so much potential yet so much holding each of them back, they kissed without reservation. Maxine clung to Isabelle's body feeling her every curve in wonderment. For what seemed like hours they touched, kissed, and swam in each other's skin. Covers twisted and pajamas scrunched up at the bottom of the bed, they lay naked, certain that it was the most natural thing in the world.

Isabelle's hands explored Maxine's body, learning what it responded to and what evoked those soft purrs from her throat. Maxine dug her fingertips into Isabelle's skin, feeling an unfamiliar desire overtake her being. Her original thought of "I don't know how much longer I can stand this" returned with a whole new meaning.

As their bodies devoured each other, Isabelle and Maxine experienced feelings that neither of them had felt before. It came in waves, increasing in frequency, until they both felt as though they would explode with the ardor mounting between them. Not letting their brains intervene, they yielded to the unknown and submitted to their first climax together. Gripping each other, long after the last swell of pleasure coursed through their bodies, Maxine finally found her voice.

"I never thought I could love anybody as much as I love you right now," she whispered into Isabelle's hair. "Have you ever felt anything like this before?"

"I didn't even know people *could* feel like this. It's a wonder anybody ever gets out of bed once they figure this out," she replied.

"But you were with Mandy, right?"

"Ah, do you have to bring that up?"

"I just wanted to know if this was new for you, too."

"It's different because it's you and I've never loved anybody who was also my best friend in the world. It's so much better this way."

Isabelle's answer satisfied Maxine's curiosity, but not her craving. Maxine began kissing down Isabelle's neck in slow circles until she reached Isabelle's breasts. She then laid her head on Isabelle's chest and stayed there until rested. Looking up at Isabelle's sleepy face, she said, "You are so beautiful. I want to see you in the light."

Isabelle unzipped the covers, sashayed to the barn door, and slid it open. Moonlight illuminated her nakedness. Maxine rose up and met her at the entrance. She slid her hands down Isabelle's skin watching the fine hairs stand at attention. Isabelle braced herself against the doorframe as Maxine kissed her. The horses nickered softly in their stables, stirred by the fever filling the barn. The rest of the night seemed timeless—their quenchless lovemaking only punctuated by short naps.

Isabelle spent her waking moments, listening to her new lover's breath rise and fall in her sleep, accompanied by an orchestra of frogs, crickets, and nightingales. When Maxine tugged Isabelle awake at sunrise, Isabelle moaned, "I want to stay here forever." Maxine looked at Isabelle, wondering how to make that wish come true.

Dark circles resided under many people's eyes at the funeral the next morning, but only Isabelle and Maxine were delightful about the origin of their own sleeplessness. Refraining from public affection was difficult, but they quelled their attraction as soon as they entered the church. Locating seats behind Erik, Maxine and Isabelle slid into the pew and sat down. Erik, wedged between his parents, twisted backwards to say hello. As soon as he saw their faces, he knew that the line had been crossed. He nodded in response to Isabelle's silent "Are you okay?"

Erik surveyed the church to see who had come to pay their last respects. There were a few kids from his school, but assumed that most of the others were from Lake Park. The Hayes family sat in the first pew, rigid and unmoving. Soon the pastor quieted down the rustlings of the audience with a loud "a-hem" into the microphone.

All heads turned in his direction and quieted down like children in Sunday school. Looking over his wire-rimmed glasses, Pastor Angeles leaned forward over the pulpit and set his eyes on the Hayes family. He parted his lips, but no sound came forward; the congregation waited. Clearing his throat, he began again. "It's never easy to preside over a child's funeral. Especially under these circumstances."

Erik could see Mr. Hayes shake his head and look down at his hands. For the duration of the eulogy, Erik kept his eyes on Jeremy's mother and father, watching their reactions to the pastor's words of consolation. Not once did they turn around to face their son's friends, teachers, and distant relatives all the way from Tuscaloosa come to find closure in an inexplicable death. Not once did they open their mouths in grief or remembrance. But their bodies spoke for them; their stiffness at the beginning of the service gradually gave way to wiltedness. Clasped hands now dangled by their sides. Taut shoulders began to slump as their backs pitched forward.

Pastor Angeles' voice rose and fell with appropriate emotion as he spoke of the young man who took his own life. Isabelle could tell that he was coming to the end of his message when he all but whispered, "He's gone. God, his Creator, weeps for Jeremy. God, the Father, mourns his lost son. God, the healer, however, can bind our brokenness and heal our wounds. We are not alone. Jeremy thought that God abandoned him. But we are the ones who abandon God. Jeremy believed that he was alone, but we are never truly alone. Jeremy chose death over life, a desperate act, an unbelievable act to those of us who remain living. Pray for Jeremy's soul."

After the pastor stepped back from the pulpit and bowed his head, the church followed suit. Only Isabelle kept her eyes open. Instead of bowing her head, she looked up at the stained glass windows searching for God. "Where are you?" she mouthed. "How can you truly exist and let this happen to him?"

A single ray of sunlight shone down through the picture of Jesus with his hands extended to his disciples. Isabelle blinked and shook her head. "I must be really desperate to be thinking this is a sign." Sign or no sign, the light remained untampered.

As the funeral ended, they waited for their aisle to file out the exit. When she and Maxine reached the door, Isabelle stopped and looked back up at the stained glass. The light had shifted and now filled the entire window. She shook her head again and let the door slam behind her.

Chapter Nineteen

The next week took on a tranquility that the year had not so far known. Isabelle couldn't believe that it was only the end of October and so much had already transpired. "This is the stuff of soap operas," she said, on the way to their first youth club meeting. "Please tell me that life is going to return to boring, old normal soon."

"Haven't there been some good things, too?"

Isabelle answered by resting her arm around Maxine's hips. "I'm grateful for you," she said. "I'd have lost all hope for the human race if I didn't have you."

"No need for that," Maxine replied.

"I'm glad you decided to come, too, Erik." Isabelle slid her free arm around his waist.

"Well, it was either this or stay home and rot."

"That's the spirit," Isabelle teased.

They walked into the church and saw about a dozen kids hanging out at some tables filled with goodies. The trio found seats next to each other and nodded hello to those near them.

"All right everyone," a girl named Jane said. "We should get started with some introductions. Tell us your name, where you go to school, and something interesting about yourself."

Reverend Kat came over and perched herself on the arm of the couch.

"I'm Jane. I go to Lakepark High and I play the saxophone."

"I'm Henry. I go to Lakepark and I have eight brothers and sisters—three who are gay, too."

"I'm Paul. I got kicked out of Foresthill High last year for spray painting the back of the gym."

"That was you?" Isabelle interrupted. "Awesome piece of work!"

"Thanks. One man's graffiti is another man's vandalism." He shrugged and smiled.

"I'm Isabelle from Foresthill High and I'm writing a play right now."

Maxine was next. "I'm Max. Foresthill, too. I live on a ranch with almost forty animals."

"Erik. Foresthill. I run cross-country."

"That's where I've seen you before," Chrissy said. "I run for Lakepark."

"Okay, I think that's everyone," Jane said, after the next few people stated their stats. "Anyone else have something to add?"

"I always got the impression from Jeremy that there weren't any other gay kids at Lakepark," Isabelle said. "He was always talking about how lonely it was there."

"Well, only a few of us hang out together. We didn't even know that Jeremy was until after...you know. Nobody talks openly about it," Trish said.

"Yeah, it's like that at Foresthill, too," Maxine joined in. "I can't believe that a couple of people from our school are here tonight." She smiled at the unfamiliar faces who might become potential friends.

"It's always somewhat shocking when you see people you know at things like this," Todd said. "And think about all the other gay people who don't have the huevos to show up. There's a ton of *them* out there."

"We've been talking about starting a GSA at our school," Isabelle said. "Do you have one?"

Jane almost jumped across the table. "We've been talking about doing that, too!"

"Maybe we should plan it now. We could do joint activities together," Maxine said.

"Can I offer a suggestion?" Reverend Kat interrupted. "Perhaps you should see what works for you here and then see how a club like this could be started at your schools."

"That makes sense," Jane said. "We can work out the kinks and do it right." She went over to an easel and flipped open the chart paper. "The agenda today is to discuss the kinds of things we'd like to do to build community. Just shout out your ideas and we'll narrow them down later."

The ideas flowed freely: "Movie nights. Dances. Ski trips. BBQs. Homeless youth outreach. Writing groups. Improv nights. Book clubs. Museum visits. Habitat for Humanity. Canned food drives."

"Let's vote on what to do first," Jane said.

"Can I put in a plug for my idea?" Paul asked.

"Sure. Go ahead."

"You may not realize it, but there's a huge number of gay kids living on the streets because they've been kicked out. I know most of us have seen the areas on Broadway where the kids hang out and pan-handle. Is anybody interested in brainstorming ways to help them out?"

Jane polled the group. "Is that okay with everyone?"

"As long as we can still plan a movie night or something just for fun," Chrissy said. The others nodded.

Mario raised his hand. "We could bring them blankets and food."

"How about doing a canned food drive?" Trish added.

Todd said, "What about collecting clothes or jackets— it's getting really cold out now that it's almost winter."

"Maybe we could set up a hotline for kids who need counseling," Isabelle piped up. "Could we set up a free line here at the church, Reverend Kat?"

There were murmurs of agreement. Paul said, "We'd have to get the information out first. Let's organize a group who will go out and let them know what we're planning."

Jane said, "Great idea! Let's hear some more options before we cement the plan, okay?"

"This may be way out there, but how about having a slumber party here at the church?" Maxine proposed, checking with Kat's expression before she went on. "We don't have to make it about God—just something for fun."

"Excellent! Then we can put together care packages like Mario, Trish and Todd suggested, before they go back to the streets," Isabelle said.

"Sounds like a good start," Jane stated. "Any other ideas before we set up committees?"

Everyone looked at each other and shook their heads. "Is this okay with you, Reverend? We've kind of just volunteered your church," Maxine asked.

"Hey, anything you guys want to do to make people's lives better, who am I to say no?" Kat said.

For the next hour, the youth group split up into four sets of trios, brainstorming and outlining the jobs that needed to be done and the timeline that they would follow. They collectively decided that they would hold the slumber party on New Year's Eve.

Isabelle, Maxine, and Erik took charge of the recruiting efforts, banking on each of their particular styles appealing to the variety of kids they might encounter. Another group planned the schedule of activities for the night, another would seek donations, and the fourth would arrange for transportation and the hotline set up.

Armed with a mighty plan, the kids talked all the way into the parking lot while Erik jotted down ideas on his notepad. "Eight weeks seems like a long time away, but we need to get started on this now if it's going to work."

"How ya doing?" Isabelle asked, as they strolled toward the curb.

"Much better," Erik answered. "When I think about what others might be going through, my life doesn't seem quite so tragic."

"Ain't that the truth?"

"Who's up for a late night movie?" Jane yelled across the parking lot. She headed in their direction, pointing down the street a little ways. "It's an art house cinema. They play a lot of weird and brainy stuff there."

Erik looked at his watch. "It's almost 10."

"Come on, let's at least see what's playing."

"Can't hurt," Maxine agreed.

Jane said, "I'll drive you home after so don't worry about that."

"Sounds good to me," Isabelle crowed.

The gaggle of new acquaintances followed their leader down the block toward the theater. As they traipsed along, the friends from Foresthill sandwiched between their Lakepark brethren, Isabelle slipped her hands into Erik's and Maxine's. She swung her arms and began to skip. Maxine fell into step and they half dragged Erik until he was laughing to the front of the theatre.

There were only three movies playing at that late hour, so the group took little time in deciding. "I sure don't want to read subtitles, and I'm not it the mood for historical drama, so it's gotta be *Nesting*," Jane said.

"What happened to 'brainy'?" Maxine teased.

Jane leaned over. "Trust me—you'll be much happier with this film."

They paid for their tickets while Isabelle called her mother to let her know they wouldn't need a ride home. Once equipped with popcorn and sodas, the kids entered the theater. Only a few other people inhabited the space, so they spread out in the middle rows and let their voices bounce off the ceiling until the movie started.

After a few requisite shushes, they settled down to watch the previews. Isabelle whispered to Erik, "Isn't this the best?"

When the movie began, all eyes fixed on the screen without wavering. The story opened with a couple going about their daily lives in New York City. They seemed to be the average, happy couple on the surface, but soon into the movie, the audience knew that something was not quite right. The man goes away on a business trip and the woman is by herself for the night. Unable to sleep, she gets dressed and walks the streets until she's cold and shivering. That's when she decides to go inside this little hole in the wall bar to get something to drink.

As she sits down in a dark booth, a woman turns around at the bar to look at her. At that moment, Isabelle shrieked, startling the entire audience.

"What's wrong with you?" Erik hissed.

She pointed at the screen. "I know her. That's Meg O'Malley. She came to my drama class a few months ago!"

"No way," Maxine said. "Are you sure?"

"Absolutely. It's that red hair."

"Be quiet. Let's see what happens," Erik said, trying to deflect the dirty looks shooting their way.

The two women make eye contact and Meg's character smiles. She lifts up her drink as though she's toasting the other woman. A few moments later, she slides off the barstool and stands in front of the woman's table and asks if she can sit down. The woman looks a little nervous, but seems to welcome the company. Once they start talking, it becomes obvious that the married woman is dissatisfied with her life and that Meg's character understands her in a way that her husband can't. The two leave the bar together and walk back to the woman's apartment.

"Is what I think is going to happen...?" Isabelle said, tucking her knees underneath her on the seat.

Maxine shushed her. "Just watch."

After some small talk on the steps, they enter the apartment and Meg's character sits down on the couch while the other woman stands by. Meg stands up and takes off her coat. Then her gloves. And then everything else. She stands completely naked in front of the other woman for a moment and then approaches her. Every eye in the theater refused to blink as the women kissed and then made love on the living room floor. There was dialogue leading up to all of this, of course, but no one could remember it once the film ended.

"I can't believe that movie," Maxine said, as they filed out the door. "I'm glad she left her husband at the end. But I felt kinda sorry for him."

"Poor guy. He really couldn't compete with that sexy redhead," Jane agreed.

"I'm trippin' about Meg still. She's so hot."

Maxine looked at her girlfriend's flushed face. "Um, don't get any ideas, okay?"

"Ideas are okay—just no action," Isabelle crushed Maxine close to her side.

"Fair enough. But I'd rather you not have any ideas, either, if you don't mind."

They piled into Jane's Camaro and deconstructed the film all the way to Foresthill. When Jane dropped them off at Isabelle's house, they said their goodbyes and made promises to talk soon.

As Erik left the girls, he pondered the surprises the evening had held. It was the first night, he realized, that Jeremy's death hadn't clouded his enjoyment of life. He noticed a lightheartedness that hadn't been there for a long time. Erik lay down in bed smiling as he recounted the club meeting, the movie, and his new friendships. "I may just be okay, after all," he said, as he turned out the light.

Chapter Twenty

Every day for the next few weeks, Erik moved closer to being okay. So much so that he decided to go to Friday's pep rally and Homecoming football game. No matter how much he begged, Isabelle and Maxine refused to accompany him. They were immersed in Isabelle's drama project and gearing up for production. Isabelle had finished the script and was gathering together a cast to film her public service announcement. Some of the church youth group had agreed to play different roles and were meeting the next morning for a dress rehearsal.

"It's perfectly okay to go alone," Erik told himself. "Maybe I'll meet up with some people I know from one of my classes."

A few hours later, he sat in the stands amidst a throng of red-and-white bedecked fans. Pom-poms flew through the bleachers like confetti and Erik found himself getting caught up in the horn blowing and spirit chants.

By halftime, the Foresthill Wildcats were up by seven and the fans were living up to their mascot's name. The crowd went crazy as the team took the field for the second half. After a nerve-wracking final quarter, Foresthill won the game by one touchdown, pushed through the end zone by none other than quarterback Mark Slater.

Erik waited until the crowds had thinned before descending the stands after the game. Nearing the edge of the bleachers, he saw a tight crowd surrounding the uniformed heroes of the evening. Erik caught Mark's white #33 on the back of his red jersey and approached the group. He stood on the fringes for a few minutes until Mark broke free from the swarm of admirers. Erik caught his eye and waved. "Just wanted to say great job out there tonight," he called over the heads blocking his access.

Mark shouldered through the mob just like he had Lakepark's defensive line and stood in front of Erik, wiping his long, sweaty bangs off of his forehead. "Hey! You came to the game!"

"You were awesome out there," Erik said. "I was so excited for you!"

"Thanks! It felt really good," Mark replied. "What are you up to now?"

"Nothing. I decided to come at the last minute."

"Then you *have* to come with me. Howie's throwing a big victory party at his house over on Westview Lane."

"I have to be home by midnight, though," Erik said, hoping he didn't sound like too big of a geek. "My dad's pretty strict."

"I'll get you home before then," Mark said. "I've got to go down to the locker room to take a quick shower. Meet me at my truck in ten minutes—you know the one, right?"

Part of him wanted to rescind his agreement to go to the party. "It's going to be full of football players and popular cliques and I may get stuck there if Mark doesn't want to take me home." Erik talked himself out of going as he reached Mark's truck in the emptying parking lot. "I better wait here to tell him, though."

Minutes later, Mark jogged up and slapped Erik on the back. "Let's go!" He opened the door to the passenger side of the cab, allowing Erik to climb over a pile of books and papers; then he went around to the other side and started the ignition. Shoving aside his concerns, Erik couldn't help but savor the musky scent of soap and cologne mingling on Mark's skin with a residue of sweat.

"Sorry, it's pretty tight in here," Mark said, as he jammed the gearshift between Erik's legs. "I'm kind of a slob." Erik pressed his back against the seat and tried to steady his body so that he wouldn't land in Mark's lap every time he turned a corner.

Erik said, "It's nice of you to invite me to go tonight."

"Hey, no problem, man. I've been thinking we should hang out. Other than just seeing each other at school for five minutes every now and then."

Erik was still puzzled about why Mark seemed interested in building a friendship with him. "Doesn't he know I'm gay? Doesn't he know I'm an outsider?" he thought. But if Mark knew, he didn't act like it. All the way to the party, he talked to Erik like he was his best friend in the world.

The pulsing music echoing off the walls of Howie's house could still be heard from the many blocks away where they'd had to park. Mark opened the front door and gently pushed Erik in front of him. A few people glanced up and began to chant: "33, 33, 33, give Mark a V for victory!" Erik stood off to the side, letting Mark have his moment. Accepting his fans adoration, Mark bowed and then clasped his hands into a mock prizefighter's fist. Someone thrust a newly tapped beer into his hand and he took a swallow. The crowd cheered again and then dispersed.

Mark set the beer down on a small end table by the foot of the stairs and said, "Come on, let's go out back." The backyard was less crowded than the rest of the house but there were still wall-to-wall people filling every crevice. Erik surveyed the scene: keg in the corner of the yard guarded by a fruit tree and three linebackers, keg in the middle of the deck surrounded by cheerleaders, and a keg on the kitchen counter with the nozzle hanging out an open window. Nearly everyone, if not everyone, had a bottle or plastic cup in hand. The louder the partiers got, the louder the music.

Mark disappeared for a few minutes and came back carrying a blue cup. He handed it to Erik. "Have some jungle juice."

Erik took a sip and said, "Tastes like Kool-Aid."

"I don't know what they put in it, but everyone seems to like it."

The two boys stood together, talking about school and sports, often interrupted by congratulations and recaps of the night's game. Mark, the king of the party, never abandoned his friend, however many girls or buddies tried to lure him away.

"You can go hang out with your friends, if you want," Erik offered at one point, motioning over to a band of athletes submerged in a hot tub a few yards away who kept calling Mark over to join them. "I'll be okay," Erik assured him. Without paying much attention, he'd drained the entire cup of jungle juice and was beginning to feel warm and uninhibited.

"Naah, I hang out with those bozos all the time. I'd rather talk to you," Mark replied.

"What's your story, Mark? Do you have a girlfriend?"

"Nope," he said, flipping his hair out of his eyes. "I did last year, but that's over now. I kind of have a thing for someone, but it's not a big deal."

Erik leaned in. "Is she here? Point her out."

Mark laughed and pushed Erik back. "Nope. It's a secret. For now at least."

Crossing his arms, Erik said, "Fine, then. I'll just have to investigate it myself." He perused the party and pointed out a brunette cheerleader who was chugging off of a beer bong, teetering back and forth on her platform heels.

"Oh please," Mark said. "Give me more credit than that. You want more juice?"

The word juice made it sound rather civilized. Feeling somewhat outside of his body, Erik heard himself answer in the affirmative. Mark took his cup and delved back into the bowels of the party, leaving Erik alone. Erik sat down on the edge of the deck and leaned back on his hands. He'd gotten used to the loud music and incessant voices around him and was actually beginning to enjoy himself. He closed his eyes and let the music wash over his body, soothing months' worth of edgy nerves.

Mark returned with another cup. They chatted for a few more minutes, and then Mark looked at his watch. "It's 11:45. I better get you home."

Erik took one more swallow and set his cup down. "Wow! Time really flew. Are you sure it's that late?" He tried to focus on his own watch but the green numbers jumped up and down out of his line of vision.

"You okay?" Mark asked. "You seem a little out of it."

"I don't feel normal," Erik slurred. "We better go."

Mark yelled goodbye to the crew outside, who protested his early departure, and led Erik through the party. The stifling heat inside worsened Erik's condition and he began to stumble. Mark braced him up and opened the door. The fresh air hit Erik like a wall of sobriety and he was able to walk by himself to Mark's truck.

"What was in that punch?" he asked, lolling his head back against the headrest in the cab. "I feel nauseated."

"You don't drink much, do you? You'll be okay in a little bit."

"Drink much? I don't drink at all. I thought that was really Kool Aid," Erik said. "I feel so stupid!"

"I just assumed you knew when I said that I didn't know what they put in it," Mark apologized. "I wouldn't have given it to you otherwise."

"You must think I'm an idiot," Erik said. "I can't go home like this."

"We can drive around a little bit 'til you sober up. What's worse—going home on time drunk or breaking curfew and being sober?"

"I guess a little bit late is better. I'm on my Dad's good side right now, so maybe he'll be okay."

"Here," Mark said, leaning over Erik and opening the glove box. As Mark's shoulder brushed up against his chest, Erik felt a rush of blood scurry up his face. With his right hand, he rolled down the window and dropped his head outside. Inhaling the fresh air calmed the nerves that surfaced as he shared this confined space with Foresthill High's star football player.

Mark dropped his cell phone in Erik's lap. "Call him and just let him know you'll be a little late."

Erik dialed the number and tried to clear his head. "Dad, I'm at a homecoming party and I'll be home a little late. The guy I came with has to drop off a couple of people before me."

"Who exactly are you with?"

"Mark Slater. And a few others from my class."

"All right. No later than 12:45, Erik. I'll be waiting up."

Erik set the phone on the seat between them. "I've got about forty-five minutes. We can't really push it past that," he informed Mark. "But I'm starting to feel a little better already. It was just so loud and stuffy in there."

Mark put the truck in gear and eased out onto the street. "I'm in the mood to drive," he said. "Where do you want to go? The park? The river?"

"Anywhere," Erik replied.

They drove without speaking for ten minutes. With the river in sight, Mark parked on the side of the road and they watched the water tumble and rush in its darkness, hurrying to some unknown destination. "Beautiful, isn't it?" Mark commented.

"It depends," Erik said.

"Oh this is where your friend...I didn't mean to be disrespectful."

Erik watched the water roll by. "It was a month ago yesterday. Seems like a year already."

"Do you know why he did it?" Mark asked.

"Not one thing, specifically. I think a lot of things contributed to it."

"You guys were best friends, right?"

"I thought so. But now I'm not so sure."

"I kind of know how you feel," Mark said. "My brother killed himself, too."

Erik shifted his body to face Mark. "He did?"

"Yeah, about three years ago. He was sixteen—my age now. It was horrible. Our family was in hell for the first year. Every holiday and birthday was so depressing. Finally, my mom made us go to therapy."

"Do you know what triggered it for him?"

"Nope. Same as your friend. Everything seemed to be wrong, in his mind. From the outside, none of us could really see, but his note left a whole bunch of reasons that

147

he considered himself a failure. Sometimes I wonder what his life was supposed to turn out like. And how his life was supposed to influence mine," Mark said.

"That's heavy," Erik said. "I'm a younger brother, too. My brother joined the Marines last year and he may be shipped off to war. So I kind of have that pressure to be the perfect son."

"I can relate. But I would never kill myself, though," Mark said. "It doesn't really solve anything."

"Well this conversation has definitely sobered me up," Erik said.

"Yeah, we can't end the night on this note," Mark agreed. "What else? Tell me something good." The way he said it reminded Erik of how Jeremy had spoken those same words to him just a few months ago, just a few blocks from this spot.

Scratching the back of his neck, Erik sat for a few minutes. A number of things swirled through his mind, none of which he felt like expressing to Mark: The way it felt when he lay in Jeremy's arms for the first time...the way the smell of men's cologne made his heart race...the way he felt right now, sitting in Mark's truck, watching the river at midnight.

"That hard to think of something good?"

"It shouldn't be, but nothing concrete is coming to mind," Erik deflected. "What about you—what do you keep on living for?"

"Don't laugh, but I love football. Everything about it. It's such a rush to play and even more to win."

"Actually, I know what you mean. Running track makes me feel like that," Erik said.

They sat staring at the river for a few more minutes, both keeping one eye on the glowing clock on the dashboard. At 12:34 a.m. Mark started the engine and let it rumble for a few minutes before pulling back onto the street. Erik gave directions as Mark drove and they pulled up in front of his house shortly before Erik's deadline. "Thanks a lot," Erik said. "And congratulations—you were really great on the field tonight."

"Thanks. I'm glad we got a chance to hang out," Mark said. "Are you sober enough to go in?" He could see a shadow lurking behind the tinted glass of the front door.

"Yeah, I'm okay now."

Mark reached over him for the second time to open the glove box and Erik allowed himself to enjoy the sensation of being close. Mark opened a pack of gum and held it out to Erik. "Just in case your father is the breath-sniffer type."

Erik stuffed two pieces in his mouth and said, "Wish me luck."

"You'll be fine. I'll see you at school on Monday, okay?"

Slamming the car door behind him, Erik jogged up to the front door and greeted his father. "Did you hear, Dad? We won the game! It was so awesome. You should have been there," Erik jabbered.

Mr. Pennington rubbed his eyes and said, "Okay son. Tell me all about it tomorrow. It's time for all of us to get some sleep."

"Sorry I made you stay up." Erik excused his lateness. "Next time I'll pay more attention to the time."

Jack led Erik down the hallway to his bedroom. "Goodnight, son. Breakfast is at nine."

The next morning, while Erik still slumbered, Isabelle gathered her crew together in the church parking lot to practice their parts. Having revised the scene she'd drafted in Mr. Kinney's class that late afternoon, Isabelle was excited to see it in action. As she equipped her actors with their scripts and blocked out the scenes, Isabelle coached them until their voices grew hoarse.

"One more time," she said, over a chorus of moans. "I promise. Then we can film it."

"My mom's picking me up in a half hour," Henry whined. "Can't we just do it now?"

"This is going to be aired at my school and maybe on national TV eventually. We can't afford to make it look amateur," Isabelle explained.

Jane said, "Let's stop complaining and just do it."

The six actors took their places in the circle and practiced one final time before Isabelle told Maxine to start rolling film. Having practiced a dozen times that morning, they executed their lines without a hitch.

Isabelle clapped her hands and crushed her actors into a group hug. "You guys kick ass!"

"Well, we had a great director," Maxine said. "I can't wait to see what it looks like on film."

"Thanks for coming, everyone. I'll show you the final cut when it's done," Isabelle said.

The next few weeks, Isabelle and Maxine holed themselves up in the back office of Outbooks, using the editing equipment Joshua had loaned them to finalize their film. They realized that cutting ten minutes worth of film into a thirty second spot was much more challenging that they could have imagined.

"I hate losing any of it," Isabelle said. "It's all necessary to get the message across."

Maxine chewed on a pencil. "Maybe we can do a series of spots instead of just one. That way we can keep all of the good stuff."

"Brilliant! You're a genius."

For the next few hours, they rolled tape and marked the places where each spot might begin and end. Joshua came in at 10:00 pm and reminded the girls that the store was closing.

"We've just finished," Isabelle announced.

"Can I see it?" Joshua asked.

"You can be our first test audience," Maxine said. "Roll tape, Izzy."

Isabelle watched his expressions change as he watched each of the three segments. When it was over, Joshua said, "That's quite powerful. And professional. I think you should send it to some networks."

"Not too controversial?" Maxine asked.

"Oh, it's way controversial," Joshua answered.

"That's the reaction I was hoping for," Isabelle said. "Thanks so much for letting us use your equipment."

"I'm just glad it's getting some use. I haven't touched it in years."

Isabelle hit eject and wrote on the label, "Master Tape. DO NOT ERASE!" She put it into her bag and stretched. "God, how long have we been here?"

"Weeks." Maxine stretched and yawned. "Let's not miss the last bus home."

Chapter Twenty-one

The latter days of November ticked away the sunny hours and replaced them with rain. The kids trudged through the wetness on their way to school with lightness in their steps. It was finally the day before Thanksgiving vacation. Christmas break would then be only moments away. Erik watched Isabelle hop through puddles in her new fluorescent pink rain boots, singing a made-up tune.

"I'm so happy it's a minimum day today!" Isabelle interrupted her song. "What time are you leaving, again?"

"Noon. Our flight's at four," Erik answered.

"You're so lucky. I wish I could come with you. Maybe you can sneak me into your suitcase."

"It's going to be a trip. I haven't seen my brother in more than a year now." Erik tallied the months in his head. "He's on a two week leave from wherever they sent him after 9/11."

"He's based in San Francisco?" Isabelle asked.

"No. He's actually stationed in San Diego, but the whole family is going to meet up in San Francisco for the holidays because it's the in-between place for all of us. My cousin Jamie is the only one who actually lives there."

"The gay one?"

"Maybe—remember, I haven't seen him in a few years. I have to say that I'm excited about seeing him again."

"I thought your Dad wouldn't set foot in San Fran 'cuz of all the dykes and fairies."

"Guess he's willing to overlook that fact because he wants to see Jack Jr. before he gets shipped out."

"What about you? You get to go the land of dykes and fairies! I'm so jealous!" Isabelle rambled as she forded a small river rushing down the gutter.

"It'd be a lot better if I wasn't there with my family," Erik said. "I know that's an awful thing to say considering it's Thanksgiving."

"You don't have to apologize. I understand."

Erik stepped onto the sidewalk while Isabelle let water flow over the toes of her boots as she made her way upstream. When they reached the shelter of an overhang near the drama building, Erik collapsed his umbrella and shook out the water onto the concrete.

Isabelle opened her hot pink slicker and reached out to hug Erik. "If I don't see you before you leave, then be sure to have a safe trip. I'll miss you." She lingered in his embrace, comforted by the smell of his shampoo. "I mean it. Be safe."

"I'll be fine, Izzy." He let her hold on until the bell rang. "These five days'll fly by. I'll call you as soon as I can. And tell Maxine Happy Thanksgiving for me."

"Anyone else I should tell?" Isabelle asked.

Erik was quiet for a minute while names rolled by like cherries in a slot machine. "No one, in particular," he said, dismissing the faces that accompanied the names. "I'll be back before anyone knows I'm gone."

153

"All righty, then," Isabelle said. "Let's get a move on." They scurried in opposite directions down slippery hallways and slid into their seats before their teachers had lowered their glasses to begin marking tardies.

"Bonjour, Madame," Isabelle greeted her teacher in a faux-French accent.

Madame Toulouse took her yardstick and tapped on the chalkboard to indicate what their assignment for the day was, and sat down at her desk, without a word in French or English.

"Man, even the teachers don't want to be here," Isabelle muttered and leaned back in her chair. She hung her head backwards and watched the rain fall up the window. Isabelle daydreamed about how Maxine and she were going to spend their break together when a form appeared in the doorway. From her upside down position, Isabelle could see clearly up the girl's miniskirt. "Who would wear a skirt on a day like this?" she asked, as her eyes traveled upward to the girl's breasts until they landed on her face. "Crap!" she said under her breath and jerked her chair upright.

Madame summoned the visitor to her desk and the two spoke in French together. Isabelle gathered from their interaction that Mandy was getting her assignments before she left for vacation. Isabelle closed her eyes and listened to Mandy's perfect accent lilt in all of the right places. "I'd forgotten about that. She does speak beautifully."

As Mandy walked towards the door, Madame called out in French, "Enjoy Paris, my dear."

"Paris! For Thanksgiving break?" Isabelle said aloud, just as Mandy reached the door. Her voice caused Mandy to pause.

"Oui," Mandy answered, and then said something in French that Isabelle couldn't interpret. She winked and was out the door.

Isabelle grabbed the wooden pass off the chalkboard tray and waved it in front of Madame Toulouse's face. "Eau du Toilette?" she asked and skipped out of the room.

Mandy was already at the end of the hallway when Isabelle called out her name. She waited until Isabelle joined her under the overhang. The rapping of the rain drowned out everything around them. "What did you say to me just now?" Isabelle asked.

"Oh, nothing. I was playing around," Mandy said.

"Playing around? We haven't talked in months and you decide to come into my classroom and 'play around' with me?"

"Don't take it so seriously, Isabelle. I'm just trying to break the ice."

"What'd you say?"

Mandy looked Isabelle in the eye and replied, "I asked if you wanted to come with me."

Isabelle's pupils dilated. "Why, in God's name, would you suggest such a thing?"

"I told you. I was being silly. It kind of popped out of my mouth. It's inappropriate. I know."

"No underlying meaning, huh?" Isabelle probed.

Mandy paused a little bit too long before saying, "Hey, I miss having fun with you. I guess that's what made me say it. I think of you when I picture Paris. That's all."

"I don't blame you—everywhere is more exciting when I'm around."

"Do you think you'll ever really forgive me?"

"Hey—it's ancient history now. I don't even remember your last name," Isabelle scoffed.

"Well, at least we're having a civil conversation. That's progress," Mandy noted.

"Yeah, well have fun in Paris. Without me," Isabelle added, throwing the bathroom pass in the air and dropping it on the way down. She kicked it like a hockey puck and watched it skid down the slick hallway.

"See ya." Mandy waved and continued in the opposite direction. Isabelle had taken no more than a few steps when she heard a crash and a scream. She whirled around and saw Mandy sitting in a pool of water just outside the front office. Rushing to her side, Isabelle asked, "Whoa—are you okay?"

Mandy held her hands out. Isabelle grabbed Mandy under her arms and lifted her to her feet. "You're soaking wet." Isabelle watched two streams of water trickle down Mandy's bare calves. "What were you thinking wearing a miniskirt in this kind of weather?" she clucked, slipping her raincoat off of her back. "Here, put this on."

"No, no, it's okay. I'll be fine," Mandy said, wiping the water off the back of her skirt.

"You look like a drowned rat! You can get it back to me after lunch. You should be dry by then. I have drama sixth period. Just bring it by Mr. Kinney's room." She draped the coat over Mandy's shoulders and stepped back. "Perfect. Now you're stylin'. Catch you later." Isabelle trotted back to French class.

"Wait, Isabelle, I'm going to..." Mandy called after Isabelle who'd already disappeared into the hallway. "...Leave before lunchtime."

After tiptoeing into the classroom, Isabelle placed the pass back on the chalkboard tray hoping Madame Toulouse wouldn't wake up from the nap she was engaged in at her desk. "What a strange encounter," Isabelle thought.

Tipping her head backwards again, Isabelle watched the rain fall up the window.

"I'll just find out where her next class is and give it to her," Mandy decided, hugging the raincoat to her soaked clothing underneath. The wetness activated Isabelle's scent and Mandy's memory of their relationship washed over her senses. Closing her eyes, Mandy let herself imagine that it was Isabelle, not her raincoat, holding and keeping her warm. The memory was so powerful, that Mandy could almost reawaken in her heart the time that they were head over heels in love.

Feeling like she was swimming in rising water, Mandy's eyes flipped open and she saw a torrent of people flooding into the hallway. She hadn't even heard the bell ring. Snapping back to reality, she fought her way upstream towards Isabelle's French class, but her old friend had been the first one out of the classroom and was long gone.

"Where's your coat?" was the first thing Maxine asked Isabelle when they met up at break. "You're freezing cold," she said, rubbing the goose bumps on her girlfriend's arms.

"Oh, you're never going to believe this..."

Just then a patch of hot pink bubbled up from the middle of a crowd on the other side of the courtyard. Maxine saw it first. "Is that who I think it is? You've got to be kidding me, Isabelle."

"This is such a bizarre story. I swear, you're gonna laugh," Isabelle began.

"Mandy Jenkins is wearing your raincoat. This should be good." Maxine's voice sounded strained.

"Honey, don't get upset. Let me tell you what happened. I was out on a bathroom pass and I saw her fall into a puddle of water. So I gave her my coat until the end of the day. It's really not a big deal. I felt sorry for her," Isabelle explained.

"That was nice. Especially considering how she treated you." Maxine folded her arms across her chest.

"Hey, you can't hold a grudge forever, right?" Isabelle said, wrapping her arms around Maxine.

Spotting the two of them across the quad, Mandy jogged over. "Isabelle, I'm glad I saw you. I was trying to tell you that I'm leaving early today, so here's your raincoat," she huffed.

"Are you dry?" Isabelle asked, dropping her arms from Maxine's waist.

"Getting there," Mandy said, shaking her watch around her wrist to see the time. "My mom's picking me up in a few minutes anyway."

"Okay, well thanks," Isabelle said. "Have fun in Paris."

Mandy replied in French and waved goodbye as she ran back over to her friends. Isabelle slid her coat on and put her arms back around Maxine. Maxine wriggled out of Isabelle's grasp and said, "Why would she say that to you?"

"Say what? You know I don't understand a word of French. I have Madame Toulouse, remember?"

Maxine was quiet for a few moments, but her contorted features revealed her anxiety. "She said, 'I'll save you a spot by the Seine.'"

Isabelle blinked. "I don't know why she would say something like that."

"You don't, huh? That seemed like a pretty personal invitation to me."

"Max, don't read into it. It doesn't mean anything."

"What am I supposed to think? She wouldn't just say that out of the blue. It seemed like she was referring to something you two had already talked about," Maxine said.

"I don't know what she's up to, truthfully, Maxine. But I have nothing to do with it," Isabelle promised.

Before Isabelle could figure out how to recount their original conversation, Maxine cut her off and said, "I've got to get to class now." She turned around and strode away. Isabelle stood alone, unsure how they were suddenly in a fight over something that shouldn't even be an issue.

Maxine sat in her Geometry class, pretending to draw planes and solve proofs. For most of the class period, however, she stewed over Mandy's unabashed attempts to win Isabelle back. "Ugh. I can't believe I'm jealous," she thought. "I can't do anything about it. If they still love each other..." The thought made her stomach queasy.

At that very moment in her English class, Isabelle was scribbling in her notebook:

I love you, not her. I have no feelings towards Mandy. She doesn't even exist in my world anymore. You're the one I want to be with and it's going to be you who I go to Paris with. And anywhere else you want to go. Maxine, I am so thankful to have you in my life and I hate to think that something stupid that Mandy said is going to come between us. Honestly, this is the first time I've talked to her in months and I can't imagine why she was saying that stuff. Maybe it was just a joke to break the ice, maybe it's something more, but it doesn't really matter what her intention was, because it makes no difference—you're the one I want. Let's forget that conversation ever happened and just enjoy our vacation together. Call me when you get home, okay?
I LOVE YOU, Isabelle

A master at escaping from class, Isabelle snuck out the door and wandered the hallways, trying to remember Maxine's room number. She finally had to settle on putting the note in Maxine's locker, knowing that she wouldn't get it until after school. On her way back to English, she saw Mandy waiting in front of the school.

Making a detour, Isabelle approached her. "What is your deal, Mandy? We don't talk for months and now you're acting all friendly."

"Just because we haven't talked, doesn't mean that I don't think about you," Mandy stated. "It feels good to be around you. I want you to consider us being friends again."

"*Friends*? Oh no. That's not going to work, Mandy. You can't just decide that you want to be around me again. I've got a girlfriend who I love and I don't want you to mess that up."

"How would I mess it up? I barely even see you around anymore." Mandy fingered the edge of her miniskirt, drawing Isabelle's eyes downward.

"Come on. Don't play dumb. You know I don't understand a word of French, but Maxine does. And she was pretty upset by your little invitation."

Mandy's smile dissolved. "I didn't mean to cause trouble. It was just a joke."

"Why do you really want from me, Mandy?" Isabelle demanded. "Let's just get this all out in the open."

"I can't say I really know. All I know is that I'm still drawn to you. It's like you're a part of me that I need. I just feel empty without you."

"You have to move on, Mandy. Figure out who you are, apart from other people. I'm not the solution to your problems. You can't just go around acting like a bull in a china shop. You're hurting people all over the place, I bet. Just stop pretending and you'll be happy. Even if people treat you miserably, you're still better off than living a lie."

Mandy smiled again. "That's what I always liked about you, Bella—your honesty. You're so strong. I don't know if I'll ever be that strong."

"Stop. I don't want to hear it. It's never going to work."

"But Isabelle. Maybe..." Mandy's green eyes sparkled with potential.

"Can you just agree to leave us alone?"

"It's not like I'm stalking you," Mandy sulked. "Don't you have room in your life for more than one person?"

Isabelle thought for a moment about the irony of the situation. "Here I am, with the most popular sophomore at Foresthill High, practically begging to be with me and I could care less. The tables sure have turned."

"Listen, Mandy, I feel for you. I'm actually sad for you. But I don't think us being friends is healthy or realistic. Remember all of the things that got in the way the first time around?"

Mandy's mother pulled up and beeped the horn twice. "Maybe, you're right, but I don't want you to be," Mandy replied, as she stepped off the curb.

"Trust me, Mandy. We're all better off this way," Isabelle said, and walked back to English class. When she grabbed the door handle, Mr. Paulson opened it from the other side. "Well, young lady, looks like you'll be spending your first day of Thanksgiving break in detention with me."

Chapter Twenty-two

The short flight only seemed long. Squashed between his father and mother, Erik kept his eyes closed in mock-sleep for the majority of the journey to San Francisco. When the pilot announced the plane's descent into the foggy San Francisco airport, Erik peered through his lids to catch his first view of the city. Ever since his parents had told him that they'd be spending Thanksgiving there, Erik had been imagining what it would be like. From his vantage point, it looked like the pilot was planning on landing in the water but, just in time, the wheels made bumpy contact with the tarmac and Erik could hear the unclicking of seatbelts clatter across the cabin.

A voice came over the staticky intercom announcing their arrival. "Welcome to San Francisco. The time is 6:36 p.m. and it's 51 degrees. You may claim your baggage at Carousel C. Happy Thanksgiving."

Erik and his parents stood in a long line to disembark and by the time they got the to baggage claim area, their suitcases were already spitting out onto the conveyor belt. "Grab the one with the red P on it," Jack called to over Erik who was still caught in a daydream. He stumbled between an elderly lady and a bodybuilder. "Excuse me, I need to get that bag." Erik pointed at the red P. The hulking man turned and smiled at him. "Let me get it," he said. The man heaved the suitcase over the head of the old lady and set it at Erik's feet. "Anything else I can do for you?" he asked and winked.

"N-n-no, th-thank you," Erik stammered and dragged the suitcase over to his father. He moved to the other side of the carousel to wait for the other bags, but found himself keeping an eye on the guy who'd helped him. Once he made accidental eye contact with the man, who smiled and nodded at him. Erik returned a quick smile. "I think I'm going to like San Francisco," he thought. "No question about it."

After the cab dropped them off at their hotel, Erik stood by the bags while his mother and father checked in. Once in the elevator, Jack handed Erik a key and said, "This is for your room. Don't lose it."

"My room? I get my own room?"

"Don't get too excited," Jack said. "We'll be next door."

Erik wheeled his suitcase to the room next to his parents' and slid the card key into the slot. A green light beckoned him in. After unpacking, Erik lay back on his bed and turned on the TV. He surfed through the channels before settling on a local news station. He was glad when the ring of the telephone interrupted a story about someone being murdered not far from his hotel. He pressed the mute button on the remote and said hello.

"Is this Erik?"

"Yes." Erik lifted up from the pillows he'd been lounging against.

"It's Jamie. I just talked to your dad and he said to call you at this extension."

163

"Jamie! Wow. I didn't expect to hear from you 'til at least tomorrow."

"Yep, it's me. I've been waiting for you to get here all week. Are you ready to go out and see the sights?"

"Right now?"

"Sure, why not? You're on vacation, aren't you?"

"I don't think my parents will go for it," Erik replied, looking at the clock. "But you can come over here and hang out with me, if you want."

"That sounds good. We can go out on the town after Thanksgiving—you're staying 'til Sunday right?"

"Yeah, maybe by then my dad will be mellower about being in the city. All the way over here in the cab he kept making sure the doors were locked," Erik reported.

"Well, I'm not too far from St. Mark's. I'll just jump on my bike and be over in about fifteen minutes, okay?"

"Sounds great!" Erik hung up and knocked on the adjoining door.

Marie opened it. "How do you like your room?"

"It's great—thank you. Um, Jamie just called, and he's gonna come over to visit me. Is that okay?"

"I don't see why not. Just don't stay up too late. Tomorrow's a big day for us. Jack Jr. will be here," his mother reminded.

Erik had almost forgotten that they'd come here to see his brother. His stomach clenched a little bit and he tried to quell the feelings rising up. Erik had been an only child for over a year now, but still had vivid memories of his brother's torture. He found himself hoping that the Marines had changed his brother for the better, but wasn't putting a whole lot of faith in the military to soften a guy.

Closing the door, Erik busied himself by tidying the already tidy room for Jamie's arrival. When he found nothing else to occupy himself with, Erik opened the bedside table and pulled out the standard-issue hotel Bible.

He flipped it open and started reading the first passage that caught his eye. Proverbs 19:20-21: "Listen to advice and accept instruction and in the end you will be wise. Many are the plans in a man's heart, but it is the Lord's purpose that prevails." Erik put his finger underneath the words to mark his place and shut his eyes.

Jamie's footsteps preceded him down the hallway and Erik shoved the Bible back into the drawer before his cousin's knock could connect with the door. He unlatched the chain and stepped back to let Jamie in. Erik took a moment to register the vision he saw before him. "Wow— you look so different!"

Jamie smiled and held out his arms. "Well, you know. I'm in art school now," he replied. "What do you think of this? I designed it myself."

He turned around to let Erik study the designs painted on his leather motorcycle jacket. Chinese characters danced along the sleeves meeting up in the middle of the back where red and orange flames consumed a long thin sword. Jamie slid his jacket off and handed it to Erik. His tight black t-shirt underneath clung to his lean torso and dark blue jeans hugged his muscular thighs.

"You just look so different," Erik repeated. "I mean, you look good, but it's obvious you don't live in Foresthill."

"I'll take that as a compliment," Jamie answered. "Living in the City has really opened up my world. I could never go back."

"Tell me what its like," Erik urged, pulling out a chair for Jamie. "All I've seen is from the window of a taxi."

"Remind me how old you are, Erik."

"Sixteen in January," Erik replied. "Why?"

"It seems like a long time since I've been sixteen and I'm only twenty now. So much has changed."

"Tell me. I've been waiting so long to talk to you."

"Well, I live in an area of town called Noe Valley with three other guys. They're all going home for Thanksgiving, so you won't meet them this trip. But you'll meet my friend Ryan. He's going to eat with us."

"We're all meeting at your house tomorrow, right?"

"Yeah, I've been cleaning and getting everything ready," Jamie said, and then slapped himself on the forehead. "Shoot, if I would've thought of it earlier, you could have stayed with me and your parents wouldn't have had to get another room. We've got two empty bedrooms this weekend."

Erik did the math. Three bedrooms, including Jamie's, and four guys living there. Two must be sharing the same bedroom. "That would be so cool!" he agreed. "Maybe you can convince my dad and I could stay over with you."

"I'll call him and suggest it so he has time to cancel your room and not get charged," Jamie offered.

"He'll be happy to save the money, I'm sure."

As if he finally had the chance to look at his cousin, Jamie said, "Look at you Erik. Almost six feet tall—and kinda buff! What have you been up to the last few years?"

"Mostly running. I do cross-country and track. I'm thinking of getting into a winter sport, too."

"You were just a peewee when I saw you last—when was it? My high school graduation?"

"Yeah, about two and a half years, I think. I was in eighth grade. Does seem like forever ago."

"Here's the big question that everyone at dinner is going to be asking you: Do you have a girlfriend?"

Erik cleared his throat. "Um, no. I'm not involved with anyone right now."

166

"Good answer," Jamie said.

"Why is that a good answer?"

"Oh, no. I didn't mean it that way. I just meant that it's a good answer to pacify our nosy family with. Noncommittal, but direct."

"Sounds like you've had some practice," Erik said. "So, what about you? Are you seeing anyone right now?"

"Yes. I am. But that's not my answer for everyone, got it kiddo?"

"Why not?"

"Because, I'm pretty sure the families wouldn't approve. I think you know what I mean, Erik."

"I understand. But you can trust me, okay? Will I get to meet, uh, this person?"

"Soon enough."

"Well, I'm looking forward to it. And I'm looking forward to staying with you. I hope my parents let me."

"I'll call them first thing in the morning." Jamie looked at the clock. "Hey, I'm supposed to meet someone at ten, so I better get going."

"I'll walk you down." Erik stashed the key card in his back pocket and held the door open for his cousin. They rode down the elevator in silence until they reached the ground floor.

"I'm parked out there." Jamie pointed to the sidewalk. "Come take a look at my bike."

Erik's mouth dropped open. "Whoa. That's awesome," he said, admiring the black and chrome Harley Davidson.

"Isn't she beautiful?" Jamie said, unhooking the helmet from the back end. "You want a ride?"

"I think I better take a rain check on that. I don't want to get into trouble this early in the trip."

"All right. There's plenty of time to get in trouble later on. See you tomorrow afternoon, Erik!" Jamie straddled the seat and gunned the engine.

"Bye," Erik called over the rumblings. "Thanks for coming over."

Jamie looked over his left shoulder and then darted out into a gap in the nighttime bustle. On his way back upstairs, Erik's mind was on overload. He got ready for bed imagining the life that Jamie was leading, hoping that he would get to see just a little slice of it during this long weekend. "Many are the plans in a man's heart..." he kept hearing over and over as he brushed his teeth and washed his face. When he lay down, he pulled the red Bible back out of the drawer and laid it on the pillow next to him.

Chapter Twenty-three

After weaseling her way out of detention with Mr. Paulson, Isabelle had walked home alone, still fuming over her conversation with Mandy and the resulting rift with Maxine. "God, this is so stupid," she said aloud to a flock of birds nestled underneath the weeping willow in her front yard. "I hate drama."

Inside, she waited and waited for Maxine to call. "I know she must have gotten my note," eventually turned into, "Maybe she never got my note." Around eight, Isabelle picked up the phone and called Maxine. Her mother answered the phone and said, "Oh honey, Maxine isn't feeling well. She went to bed about an hour ago. I'll let her know you called."

Isabelle wanted to say, "That's not true. She's just mad at me. We need to clear things up. Please let me talk to her." But she didn't. Maxine's parents still didn't know the nature of their daughter's relationship with her best friend and Isabelle didn't want to worsen the situation by revealing any information that she wasn't supposed to. She had no choice but to accept Maxine's refusal to talk to her.

Lying back on her bed, Isabelle fought the destructive impulses rumbling inside of her. "What did Nancy tell me?" She tried to remember the strategies her therapist had suggested to stay above water when she felt like drowning. She picked up the phone again to call Erik this time and listened to the empty rings echoing down the street in his empty house. "Oh yeah," she remembered. "He's gone, too." Before allowing herself to get depressed, she thought of what she could do to make things better with Maxine.

"Okay, so maybe I did take things a little far by pursuing Mandy out into the hallway the first time or by giving her my coat," Isabelle reflected. "I guess I'm just a sucker for female attention."

She got up and walked into her mother's study and stood in the doorway. "Hey Ma."

"Hi Izzy, what's up?" Ana took her reading glasses off and looked at her daughter. "Uh-Oh. What's wrong?"

"How do you always know when something's wrong?" Isabelle grumbled.

"Mother's intuition. Or it could be the fact that you don't have a phone sticking to your ear and Maxine isn't over here."

"Pretty transparent, aren't I?"

"Did you two have an argument?"

Isabelle summed up what had happened at school that day while her mother listened without interruption.

"Well, maybe it was a misunderstanding, but Maxine's clearly hurt if she won't even talk to you. Why don't you think of something special to do for her so she knows that she's the one you want?"

Isabelle's head, which had been leaning against the door frame, perked up. "Like what?"

"You're the most creative person I know. You'll think of something. Just dig around the house and see if anything piques your interest."

"Do you think it'll help?"

"Well, I can't say what Maxine's reaction will be. It may take awhile for her to trust you again if she thinks things aren't over with Mandy. But if you make a good faith effort, it certainly can't hurt the situation."

"Mom, I don't know how you know the things you do, but I'm glad."

"Sweetie, I've made my share of mistakes, believe me," her mother replied. "That's where wisdom comes from."

"I suppose I'll be very wise one day," Isabelle thought, as she wandered from room to room finding nothing that inspired her. Frustrated, she walked outside onto the back porch and sat down. Head in hands, her earlier excitement had faded. "Tomorrow's Thanksgiving and she won't even see me," she lamented. "Thanksgiving—of all days!"

When she lifted her head, Isabelle saw something that she hadn't noticed before. There were three small trees sitting in a row of black plastic pots with the price tags still on them. The saplings were about five feet high covered in tiny leaves on tiny branches jutting out from all sides. "Where did those come from?" she wondered. Squatting down to examine the tags, Isabelle read, "Jacaranda. Gingko. Chinese Pistache." She wrapped her forefinger and thumb around the trunk of the Pistache and felt its smooth bark. "Perfect!"

"Mom!" she yelled to the window over the deck.

Ana peered through the shutters. "What are you doing out there, Isabelle?"

"I have a huge favor to ask. Please say yes."

"What is it?"

Isabelle pointed to the trees sitting at her feet. "Can I have one of these to give to Maxine?"

"A tree?"

"Wait 'til you see what I'm going to do with it! Please, Mom. I'll buy you another one. I just want to have this one tonight so I can deliver it to Maxine on Thanksgiving."

Ana sighed. "You know I always say yes, Isabelle."

"I know, Mom. That's the way it should be."

Lugging the tree over to the sliding glass door, Isabelle met up with her mother. "Just one request," Ana said. "Don't drag it through the house. Can you work out here?"

Isabelle thought of her plan and agreed. "I can do the first part inside and then assemble it out here later on."

Trotting back to her room, Isabelle dug under her bed for her art supplies. She found a stack of homemade paper she'd made over the summer in her art class. Flipping through the rough multicolored pages imprinted with leaves and flowers, Isabelle pulled out a few of her best pieces and set them on the floor. She then gathered up scissors, calligraphy pens, and a roll of hemp twine and began construction.

Isabelle cut the paper into triangles and then folded them over into small cards. She then pricked a hole in the edge of each one and wove a piece of twine through the puncture. On each card, she wrote in calligraphy the things she was thankful for:

Thankful for your friendship.
Thankful for your inner beauty.
Thankful for your understanding.
Thankful for your loving kindness.
Thankful for your presence in my life.

172

Thankful for your forgiveness.
Thankful for your contagious laughter.
Thankful for your creativity.
Thankful for your sweet, sweet spirit.
Thankful for the brightening my every day.
Thankful for YOU!

After she'd written about thirty different messages, Isabelle gathered up the drying cards and carried them to the back door. The kitchen clock notified her that it was almost midnight, but Isabelle refused to sleep until her gift was complete. She slid the door open and turned the porch light on. It illuminated the whole back yard, so Isabelle flicked it off. She opened up the pantry door and grabbed a flashlight instead.

Propping the flashlight up against a planter-box, Isabelle began tying the cards to the budding branches. The cards fluttered like luminous leaves dangling from the limbs. She made sure as to not damage any of the real fledgling leaves poking their miniscule green arms and legs from the twigs. When she was finished, Isabelle stepped back to examine her handiwork.

Isabelle rubbed her numbing hands together and watched her breath crystallize in the air around her. Though reluctant to leave her creation, she decided that she'd better go in and warm up or she'd end up catching a cold for vacation. Warming a cup of hot cocoa in the microwave, Isabelle stared out the window at the tree. They'd never been in a fight before and the feeling gnawed at Isabelle to the core. She couldn't imagine life without Maxine and hoped that she wouldn't have to.

As soon as daylight broke its way through her window blinds the next morning, Isabelle popped out of bed. Even though she'd only gotten a few hours of sleep, she was more alert and energetic than usual. After cajoling her mother through a cup of coffee, Isabelle and Ana loaded the sapling into the back seat of the car and drove to Maxine's house.

"I just want to leave it on her porch," Isabelle said as they wound through the country road to the ranch. When they arrived, Isabelle tried to hush the crunching tires on the Kotamo's gravel driveway. "I don't want to wake them up," she whispered to her mother, knowing that Maxine's family was always up before the sun to feed the animals.

Ana put the car in Park but left the motor running. They carefully extracted the tree and righted it on the porch near the front door. Isabelle untangled the twisted cards and shook the branches a little bit to fluff them out. "What do you think?"

"You've really outdone yourself, Isabelle."

"Okay, let's go. I think we made it."

As Isabelle and Ana climbed back into the car and pulled towards the street, Maxine removed her eyeball from the peephole. As soon as she could no longer hear their car, Maxine opened the door and reached out to touch the flickering pieces of paper on the branches. Her fingers separated the two halves of one card and read the message:

Thankful for your forgiveness.

Maxine made her way around the limbs reading each card and then smuggled the tree into her bedroom. She placed it in a corner by the window and watched the sunlight dance on the branches. There she sat for twenty minutes, allowing her bitterness to thaw. Maxine dialed

Isabelle's number without taking her eyes off the tree. "You drive me crazy," she said, when Isabelle answered.

"Is that a good thing?" Isabelle gripped the receiver. "Listen Maxine..."

"No, Isabelle, you listen," Maxine commanded and Isabelle obeyed, her mouth frozen in almost-speech. "First of all, if you love me and want to be with me, then you have to respect me. Even though I'm hopelessly in love with you and want to be with you more than anything, I *will* get out if you think this is a just a game. You're going to realize one day, Isabelle, that you are desirable, beautiful, and worth fighting for, and a lot of people are going to want to be with you. But you need to decide right now if you want all that attention from the world or if you want it from me. I hate to give you an ultimatum, but that's how I feel. Now you can talk."

Isabelle remained stunned for a few moments. As she fully soaked in what Maxine had just declared, she replied, "I choose you. That's all."

"You sure, Isabelle? There are a lot of women out there who are going to turn your head. And vice versa—I'm not going to spend my life fighting women off of you."

"Well, what about you? What happens when you realize how amazing and incredible you are? Maybe I'm the one who should be worried..."

"Let's be realistic. We don't live in a bubble. Sure, there are going to be lots of people who come our way, but what we have to decide right now is how we're going to react when they do. Are you up for this, Isabelle? Do you want to be in a relationship with me right now?"

Without giving Isabelle a chance to answer, Maxine's tone changed. "Maybe we're just too young to decide to be with each other exclusively. I can't *make* you decide you're never going to be attracted to anyone else. For God's sakes, we're only fifteen."

"What are you saying? Max, you're not breaking up with me."

Maxine was quiet for about a minute, leaving Isabelle hanging. "No. I'm not. I don't want to. I'm just scared. What happens if our feelings change?"

"I'm sure they will," Isabelle answered. "But that's natural. Our relationship will change as we grow up, but that's no reason to stop it now. Don't you want to take the risk? Aren't we worth it?"

"Yesterday, I got a glimpse of what I might have to deal with being with you and part of me just wanted to give it up. When I saw Mandy wearing your coat, I just wanted to lose my mind. And know what was worse—the absence I felt those twelve hours that we weren't talking. Isabelle, I'm in over my head and I don't know what to do," Maxine said, her initial resolve vanishing.

"Honey, I can only tell you this: you are the most important person in my life and I don't want to risk losing you. Can you give me another chance to show you that you're the one I want?" Isabelle pleaded. "What do I have to do? I'll do it."

Maxine looked at the tree. "You spent a lot of time on it, didn't you?"

"Most of the night. But I enjoyed every minute of it because it brought me close to you when I couldn't be in real life."

"It's beautiful. I've never gotten such a wonderful gift." Maxine fingered the soft buds.

"It's not half of what I feel towards you," Isabelle said. "I wish it could tell you what I was feeling when I was working on it."

A breeze came through Maxine's window and ruffled the cards. As they murmured amongst themselves, Maxine thought, "How did she do that?"

"Are we okay?" Isabelle asked. "Can I see you?"

Maxine swallowed and cleared her throat of the emotion settling there. "Oh Isabelle, what am I going to do with you?"

"I'll take that as a yes," Isabelle chirped. "When can you come over?"

"Well, all of my relatives are coming for Thanksgiving this afternoon, so it won't be until tonight."

"Same situation here. See if you can spend the night later on, okay?"

"All right, Bella. I'll call you later."

"Hey Max, guess what?"

"What?"

"I love you."

"You better. If you think I was mad today...well, just don't push it."

"All right. I hear you loud and clear. Hey, I better get going—it's my job to defrost the Tofurky." Isabelle hung up the phone to Maxine's giggles and hummed a tune as she entered the kitchen.

Ana looked up from the cutting board and smiled at her daughter. "All is well?"

"All is well."

Chapter Twenty-four

"Isabelle's not going to believe this!" Erik thought as he followed his cousin's lead on a tour through the flat before dinner was served.

The design on the back of Jamie's motorcycle jacket was tame in comparison to the décor of the apartment. Each room was decorated with a different motif—the kitchen held a rustic flavor that yielded to a wilder African-themed dining room next door. The bedrooms were adorned in the personal style of each inhabitant; Erik captured a snapshot of Jamie's missing housemates. One of them was apparently obsessed with jazz, the other a sports fanatic, and Jamie's room was swathed in Oriental art and silk wall hangings.

The tour ended in the living room, which reminded Erik of the Art Deco era, with its red chaise lounge, high backed couches, and 1920s photographs. The extended Pennington family sat on the furnishings, feeling as odd as the rooms in the house.

Jack Jr., however, was the man of the hour—the aunts and cousins all clucking over him as he regaled them with his military tales, while his father beamed nearby. Erik slipped out and joined Jamie in the kitchen. "Can I help?" he asked, leaning against the doorway. "I know you said that no one was allowed in the kitchen, but..."

"You're the exception. I just didn't want all those Pennington women in here telling me how to cook." Jamie grinned at Erik.

"I can't believe my father actually agreed to let me stay here. I hope he doesn't change his mind after..." Erik stopped mid-sentence.

"After seeing my crazy house?" Jamie finished for him. "It's okay. I'm not offended."

"I like it here," Erik said. "But you know how conservative my family is."

"Yeah, somehow you got all the right-wing genes—my dad's side ended up being more liberal." Jamie looked Erik up and down. "Yup—you're the perfect preppy. Not a hair out of place."

"I try not to stand out. I guess it works."

"Why not stand out? What else is there to do?"

"If I wasn't living in Foresthill, I might be more open to the idea. Being different just means you're more likely to get your butt kicked."

"I know. It's easy for me to say. I don't have to live there anymore."

Erik nodded and leaned back against the cabinet, feeling more at home in Jamie's kitchen than most other places he'd been in his life. "You're lucky to have all this."

"Yeah, I am. Wait 'til you meet Ryan. He should be here soon." Jamie said, glancing at the clock on the oven.

"Tell me about him. Where did you meet?" Erik decided to just act as if Jamie had already come out to him and Jamie followed suit.

179

"It sounds so cliché, but we met at this little coffee house in Berkeley called Café Au Lait. He was sitting in a corner reading this enormous book, so I went up to him and asked what it was."

"And?" Erik asked, lifting himself onto a stool.

"He looked at me with this calm expression behind these adorable wire-rimmed glasses and closed the cover of the book so I could read the title: *Legal Foundations of Case Law*."

"He's a lawyer?"

"Berkeley Law. He's in graduate school. To tell you the truth, I don't know what he sees in me. We're complete opposites. He's a total brain and I'm, well, you know—I'm unique," Jamie concluded. "You two should get along well."

As if on cue, the doorbell rang and Erik slid off the stool, trailing Jamie as he scampered to the door. Erik waited for Jamie to lead Ryan inside before sticking out his hand to greet him. "It's good to finally meet you," Erik said to the handsome man who commanded the room by his very presence. "Jamie was just telling me..."

"That he should get back into the kitchen and finish making that garlic bread," Jamie said. Then he whispered, "You two can talk after everyone's either passed out or gone home, okay?"

Ryan linked his arm through Erik's and said in a smooth accent that Erik couldn't identify, "I think we're making him nervous." The muscular arm brushing against Erik's side caused minor tremors across his skin.

"Come on, Ryan. You can help me with the difficult task of buttering the bread," Erik said.

"I think I can handle that," Ryan said, flexing his bicep. They walked into the kitchen, bantering back and forth like old friends until dinner was ready.

180

Once Jamie had herded everyone into the dining room for dinner, he stood at the end of the table and clinked his glass with a fork. As the room hushed, Jamie toasted his family. "Welcome to Thanksgiving at my home. It's such a wonderful gift to have all of you here. We're especially thankful to have Jack Jr. with us for the holidays. I hope you all enjoy your stay in San Francisco. Bon Appetit!"

For the next few minutes, conversation subsided as the Pennington family served and devoured the turkey, broccoli casserole, stuffing, yams, and pumpkin pie. As they pushed themselves back from the table in satisfaction, the family noticed that there was someone at the table unrelated to them.

"Ryan?" Jack Sr. began. "How do you know Jamie?"

"I guess we've known each other about a year now." Ryan crafted his answer. "I live just a few blocks away."

"Where are you from?" Jack continued.

"Africa, actually. I was born here in the City but my family moved to South Africa when I was six," Ryan said. "I came back here a few years ago to attend graduate school."

The other dinner conversations settled like dust after a windstorm, everyone interested in hearing what the outsider had to say. "That's where your accent is from," Jack Jr. stated. "There's a guy in my platoon from South Africa. He's white, though."

Erik cringed at his brother's comment. But Ryan just laughed. "Well, there are white people in Africa, too. Some of my best friends are even white." Ryan winked at Jamie.

"How can he be so easygoing?" Erik wondered. "It's one thing to be the only non-family member at the table, but to be black, foreign, and gay—how does he handle it?"

"Can I get anyone anything?" Jamie broke in, attempting to save Ryan from the third degree.

"Sit down, Jamie. Enjoy yourself," Ryan entreated. "It's not every day that you get to spend time with such a wonderful family. Now, Jack, tell me about *your*self."

Jack leaned forward and accepted Ryan's request. One by one, each family member stole out of the dining room and soothed him or herself by the crackling fire in the front room. Thirty minutes later, when only Erik, Ryan and Jack remained, Ryan suggested that he and Erik go help Jamie clean up in the kitchen.

"Women's work," Jack protested. "Marie?"

"Oh no, sir." Ryan held up his hand. "In my culture, it's honorable for the men to clean up after the meal has been finished."

Jack waved them off and slung his head back into a snore. Erik burst into giggles when they reached the sanctity of the kitchen. "Is that true? What you just told my father about African men?"

"African men? Oh, no, Erik—they're about as sexist as it gets! I was talking about gay men." Ryan jutted out his hip and snapped his fingers in the air.

Jamie chuckled. "Can you tell that he's a lawyer?"

Erik dried the dishes as Ryan passed them to him. "You were right, Jamie. Ryan and I will get along just fine."

Within an hour, the rest of the visitors drifted back to their own lodging, leaving just Erik, Jamie, and Ryan in the apartment. Before Erik's parents returned to their hotel room, they left their son with strict instructions to call them in the morning.

The next morning, Erik woke up under a thick Afghan among half a dozen pillows, almost forgetting where he was. Propping himself up on an elbow, he surveyed the now clean living room where he'd fallen asleep the night before. He could hear the clinking of glasses and running water in the kitchen couched with soft voices and a burbling coffee pot.

"Hey sleepyhead," Jamie said, as he entered the room to pick up a few more stray glasses. "Were you comfortable last night? We were worried you'd wake up all twisted from sleeping on that couch."

"I don't even remember falling asleep," Erik said, with a yawn. "I must've been wiped out."

"Yeah, we were just hanging out talking and you fell asleep about ten minutes into it."

"Shoot—did I miss anything good?"

"Ryan?" Jamie called into the kitchen. "Did Erik miss anything good from last night's conversation?"

Poking his head around the corner and slinging a damp towel over his broad shoulder, Ryan replied, "Oh yeah, we talked all about you."

Erik sat up straight. "No you didn't."

"Bet you wished you stayed up, huh?"

"That's not fair. What were you saying?"

"Join us in the kitchen and we'll tell you over breakfast and coffee."

"Do I have time to shower?" Erik asked, smoothing the wrinkled dress pants he'd inadvertently worn as pajamas.

"Go ahead. But I'm making banana pancakes, so snap to it," Ryan responded.

Erik grabbed his bag from the jazz room where he was supposed to have slept and made his way to the bathroom. He couldn't believe how at home he felt and gratefully counted his three more days of staying there. After showering and pulling on a new pair of jeans and a white turtleneck sweater, Erik walked into the kitchen and said, "Good morning. Smells great in here!"

"You look nice, Erik," Jamie said, and then to Ryan in a Southern accent, "Isn't he the cutest little preppy you ever did see?"

"Adorable," Ryan agreed. "So honey, tell us the truth. We've been speculating all night about you."

"What do you want to know?"

"Everything. I was just chastening Jamie—he barely knows you at all. He was useless when I tried to pump him for information."

"I try not to pry," Jamie said.

Over breakfast, Erik told them about his town, his family, Isabelle, running track, and other facets of his life, but left the topic of Jeremy waiting in the wings. "See, I'm not that interesting," he finished.

Ryan, who had been nodding politely and storing all of this new information in his brain, said, "Well, you've covered it all, except your love life."

"I don't have one," Erik stated.

"No one? I can't believe a catch like you doesn't have someone interested." Ryan flattered Erik into answering.

"Well, I'm just getting over somebody right now," Erik admitted. "We were together for about five months, which isn't that long, I know, but we had something special."

"Why'd you break up?" Jamie asked.

The room was silent while Erik decided whether to respond. Clearing his throat, he answered, "Suicide."

Ryan reached over and covered Erik's hand with his own. "I am so sorry, Erik. What a terrible loss for you."

Jamie walked over and lifted Erik out of the chair and into his arms. Ryan stood up and hugged Erik from the other side. The warmth of the gesture took Erik off guard. He allowed himself to receive the love and found the pain he'd been harboring almost dissolve.

"It feels good to share this with you. I write about it sometimes, but haven't really talked about it since it happened," Erik said when they released him.

"Well, you've been through hell. You don't have to tell us the details if it's too fresh, but we'd like to help you through this," Ryan said.

"I appreciate it. But I'm really doing okay—surprisingly okay. I'd rather just have fun with you guys this weekend."

"Then, I've got a super-duper idea," Jamie said. "Why don't we go shopping?"

"It's the day after Thanksgiving. It'll be crazy out there," Ryan protested.

"Please, please, please..." Jamie hopped up and down like a five-year-old waiting to see Santa Claus. "We can just walk down to the Castro. I won't drag you to Embarcadero where all the breeders are. Please..."

"You game?" Ryan asked Erik.

"Sure. I've never been to the Castro, but Isabelle told me about it."

"Oh it's a trip. I think it may be just what the doctor ordered for you," Ryan said.

"Last one ready has to buy me lunch," Jamie yelled, and dashed to the bedroom to get dressed.

"I always end up buying him lunch anyway. I guess that's what being in love gets me, huh?"

Erik said, "He's a lucky guy. You both are. I just hope one day..."

"You will, Erik. You will."

185

Chapter Twenty-five

"I still can't believe this place is for real," Erik said for the tenth time. "Look at all these people. Men holding hands. Rainbow flags everywhere."

Jamie and Ryan, holding hands themselves, just laughed. "We knew this would blow your mind. I remember the first time I came here," Jamie said. "I thought I'd died and gone to heaven."

"And nobody even blinks an eye. It's like we're all totally normal here—the straight people kinda look out of place," Erik said, referring to the few straight couples shopping alongside their gay brothers and sisters.

"Yeah, it's one of the few places in the world where we're safe," Ryan said. "*Well*, safer than usual. There are the homophobes who sometimes come down here to bash us. But that's not too common in this particular area."

As they strolled down Castro onto Market, wandering in and out of boutiques and bookstores, Erik felt more relaxed than he had in years. Laden with bags of trinkets and gifts, the three decided to stop for lunch at Café Flora. Once seated in the heated patio area, Erik ordered his meal and proceeded to people watch while Jamie and Ryan discussed their plans for Christmas break. His eyes couldn't get their fill of this seemingly-gay parallel universe. Lesbians, gay men, transgendered drag queens, couples with children, people of all different races walking dogs of all different breeds, elderly folks, and bands of teenagers filled the streets, with a sense of coexistence and unity that Erik only dreamed of.

It was the latter group that Erik was particularly interested in. Though most of the young people he saw were more Isabelle's funky style that his, Erik was overjoyed to see boys with arms draped over each other and girls linked elbow to elbow. Jamie and Ryan continued their conversation, noticing that Erik hadn't touched his food by the time the bill came.

"Just wrap it up," Erik said. "I think I'm still full from last night."

"Liar. You're just boy-crazy. Look at you," Jamie remarked. "Can't keep your eyes off the streets."

"I know. I'm obsessed."

"Leave the boy alone. He's just having a Castro experience," Ryan interjected.

Just then, a young man with a long, red scarf walked by the café and paused at the posted menu. The boy's flaxen hair curled out from under his red cap framing a doll-like face with ruddy cheeks and curling eyelashes over two round blue eyes. As Erik watched his full lips read over the menu, he imagined himself being the recipient of those words. Shaking his head, Erik pried away his glance.

Jamie and Ryan stared in the same direction with grins on their faces. "Just your type, eh?" Ryan nudged Erik's side.

"Let's go meet him, then," Jamie suggested.

Erik swiveled around. "Are you nuts? I can't just walk up to a total stranger and pick up on him."

Jamie's laughter was so loud that the boy at the menu averted his gaze and found himself focusing on the table of three good-looking men gawking at him. He disappeared into the restaurant.

Erik's voice rose. "Is he coming out here, do you think?" He looked back to the empty space where the man had left the menu.

"Guess we'll soon find out," Ryan said. "We'll wait a few seconds and see what happens."

"Why am I getting so worked up over a guy that I don't even know? Maybe Jamie's right—I'm just boy-crazy." As Erik swallowed a few deep breaths to slow the pounding of his heart, he said aloud, "Come on. I'm ready to go now."

"You sure?" Ryan asked.

"Totally. Where are we off to next?"

Jamie flipped open an imaginary brochure and moved his finger down an invisible agenda. "Hmm...looks like we're ready for North Beach."

"You want to travel across the City?" Ryan asked. "I thought we were just hanging out in the Castro today."

Grabbing Ryan's wrist and looking at his watch, Jamie replied, "Well, it's only 2:00—don't you think we should show Erik as much of the City as possible?"

Ryan turned to Erik and inquired, "What do you want to do?"

"Is North Beach like it is here?"

"Not really. It's kind of like Little Italy and Chinatown mixed together with a dash of bohemians and beatniks." Jamie painted the scene. "But don't worry, honey, there's gay people all over this city. Plus, we'll be back here tonight. Then you'll really see the Castro!"

"Okay. I'm sold. How do we get there?"

"Muni. Three of us can't fit on my bike," Jamie said.

Their conversation was interrupted by a charming voice. "Do you mind if I borrow some sugar from your table?" The man held up the sweetener holder from his own table. "Mine only has Equal."

Erik turned his head and found himself looking right into a bright red scarf. His eyes traveled up the scarf to the neck it was wrapped around and then to the lips speaking the words. Without taking his eyes off the young man's face, Erik's hand waded over the topography of the table, picked up the container, and handed it to the visitor.

"Thank you," he said, smiling down at Erik and then returning to his table. Erik watched him stir two packets of sugar into his tea and blow on the steam before taking a sip. Jamie and Ryan waited for Erik to decide what he wanted to do. Then, before they could ask him, Erik was already in motion towards the young man.

"Hi, I don't mean to interrupt you, but do you know the City well?" Erik asked, putting his hands in his pockets to hide their shaking.

"Lived here all my nineteen years," the young man answered. "What can I do for you?"

"Well, my cousin and his friend over there suggested that we go to North Beach on Muni and they can't remember which bus to take. Do you know?"

"That's an easy one. Just get on the one that says Chinatown/North Beach and it'll drop you off right on Columbus."

"Oh, that is easy." Erik wished he'd come up with a better question.

"Where are you from?" the stranger asked, as he took a swallow of tea.

"A little town called Foresthill. I'm just here for the holidays. I've never been to San Francisco before. But I love it so far!"

"Then you should have a guided tour. Patrick Mason at your service," he said, taking another gulp. "Do you mind if I tag along?"

"Really?" Erik said. "That'd be fun."

"Sure. I had nothing to do today except hang out here and study. Wandering around the City with some new faces sounds like a great distraction," Patrick said.

"What are you studying?" Erik asked.

"I'm in my second year at SF City College. I think I'm leaning towards majoring in Film Studies, but I'm not sure yet. I still have a penchant for horticulture. Funny, huh?"

Erik swooned at the word "penchant". "That's pretty unique," he replied, as Patrick took his last swig and placed a dollar underneath the saucer.

"Okay, let's go. The day is young."

The two walked over to Jamie and Ryan and exchanged introductions. "Looks like we have our fourth," Jamie said.

They walked to the nearest Muni stop, talking about the City, their lives, and who they knew in common. Erik stood by, wishing that he was part of the community they spoke of. Once seated next to each other, Patrick inundated Erik with questions. Erik answered selectively, omitting the fact that he was still in high school and living in his parents' home.

"What are you studying in school?" Patrick asked.

"A little bit of everything," Erik answered. "But history is really my focus."

"What are your future plans?"

"As a history major? That's the big question. Probably a teacher or maybe a college professor."

"I can just imagine you wearing one of those tweed blazers with the brown patches on the elbows. How cute!" Patrick flirted.

Erik's face matched Patrick's red scarf. "I'm pretty easy to peg, eh?"

"Not at all. When I first saw you, I didn't know if you were gay. Wait—are you gay?" Patrick deadpanned.

Laughing, Erik answered, "Yes" for the first time in his life with joy. The Muni bus groaned and grumbled over the San Francisco hills and finally wheezed into the Columbus and Green station. They got off the bus and followed Patrick's lead down to City Lights Bookstore.

"This is where Ferlinghetti and Kerouac hung out in the sixties. You'll dig it here." Patrick held open the door.

The old wood creaked under their feet and, at various places in the store, Erik had to duck his head under a beam to enter the mysterious rooms drowning in the printed word. "I can't even figure out what to look for." Erik's eyes surveyed the chaotic organization.

"Just explore," Patrick said, leaving him to browse through a bin of .99 cent books near the back corner. After about an hour of delving into the shelves of room after room, Erik ended up back at the front counter with half a dozen books in his arms. He sifted through them, deciding which ones he could live without before plopping the other three onto the counter.

"What'd you get?" Patrick appeared out of nowhere.

"I could barely decide. I'd love to buy the whole store," Erik answered, handing the clerk his money. "But I settled for a couple of books I could read and then pass on to my best friend Isabelle."

"It's a great place, huh?"

"Yes. Thanks for bringing me here."

"The pleasure's all mine," he said, squeezing Erik around his upper arm.

"He wants to be close to me. He likes me." It finally dawned on Erik.

On the sidewalk outside, Jamie and Ryan discussed that very topic. "Can you believe it? The boy's in the City for two days and he meets a sweetie like that. I was here a whole year before I even met another decent human being," Jamie said.

"I'm just as shocked as you are. Erik's so darn shy. I never thought he'd actually go up and talk to him."

"I just hope he doesn't fall in love in one day and then get his heart broken when he has to go home."

"Well, we can't control any of that. Let's just let him enjoy his day."

The young men walked out of the store, each carrying a bag. "Ready to go on the next adventure?" Patrick asked. "This way."

They led the trek up the hill to Coit Tower, while Ryan pulled a whining Jamie up the steep grade a good pace behind them. Once atop the hill, Patrick led Erik to a spot overlooking the Golden Gate Bridge and the San Francisco Bay. He placed Erik in front of him and put his hands on his shoulders while he pointed out various landmarks.

Erik lost him after Patrick said, "There's Alcatraz," and could only focus on the warmth of Patrick's breath in his ear and the heaviness of his hands on his shoulders. Erik found himself leaning back into an almost-embrace while Patrick outlined the history of the area. Pretending that the wind whipping against his face was what was causing him to shiver, Erik sank deeper into Patrick's chest. Patrick unwove the long scarf and rewrapped it so that it enveloped both of them.

By now, Jamie and Ryan had made it to the top and were watching the attraction develop between the boys. "What a darling picture," Jamie gushed, digging into his knapsack for his camera.

Soon the biting wind was enough for everyone, and they descended down the hill in search of a cup of coffee. Patrick slipped his hand into Erik's coat pocket and locked fingers with him as they trotted down the decline. Though the feeling excited him, Erik knew that he needed to tell Patrick the truth. He already liked him too much to want to mislead him. But as the day drew on, Erik never opened his mouth to elaborate on the important information he'd left out of their earlier conversation.

As evening faded into night, Patrick stuck by Erik's side, until they reached Jamie's apartment after midnight. Jamie and Ryan slipped inside, leaving the boys alone on the front steps.

"Here, I have something for you," Patrick said, digging into one of his shopping bags. He pulled out a hardcover book and handed it to Erik.

Erik flipped it over and read the title: *The Giving Tree* by Shel Silverstein. "I love this book. I used to have it when I was younger. You're so thoughtful, Patrick!" Erik leaned over and kissed him on the cheek.

Now it was Patrick's turn to blush. "You're welcome. It's different when you read it as an adult."

Erik blanched. "I'm barely an adult now," he thought. "Listen, I need to tell you something Patrick."

"What is it?"

"Well, I've wanted to tell you something all day, but I didn't want to ruin it."

"Don't tell me. You already have a boyfriend."

"No, that's not it." For a split second, an image of Mark flashed through his mind. He shook his head to free himself of the ridiculous thought. Erik said, "But I have slightly misrepresented myself."

Patrick waited for Erik to continue.

"I'm younger than I've led you to believe. I'm still in high school, Patrick. I'm sorry I didn't tell you earlier. I just liked you so much."

"Well, that's not that big of deal. I've only been out of high school a year now myself. How old are you?"

"Sixteen in January," Erik answered.

Patrick dropped Erik's hands and rubbed his together. "A sophomore?"

"I'll understand if you don't want to see me again. I wish I was older, but there's nothing I can do about it. You know what I mean?"

"Yeah, I know. I just don't want to be a cradle robber. And there's also the fact that you don't live anywhere near here. Maybe we should just call it a day, huh? I really enjoyed meeting you Erik. You're a great guy," Patrick finished. "Maybe we'll meet again one day."

"Can I at least have a hug goodbye?"

Patrick smiled and opened his arms for a last embrace. The two clung together until their attraction threatened to erase their words, and then let go. "Bye Erik," Patrick said. "Have a safe trip home."

Erik waved and leaned against the porch railing until Patrick's red hat and scarf were out of sight. Then he sat down on the porch and opened *The Giving Tree*. Inside, Patrick had inscribed these words: "Give and it shall be given unto you."

Turning to page one, Erik began to read aloud. When he finished the whole story, he sat back against the steps and savored the gifts of the night.

Chapter Twenty-six

A few days later, Erik returned home, where he filled in an eager Isabelle on his San Francisco adventures. Winter descended onto Foresthill and his memories of the boy in the red scarf remained fond. Often he thought of Patrick's deep blue eyes and that coy smile, wondering where he was and what he was doing. Erik hadn't talked to Jamie since they said goodbye at the airport, promising to keep better in touch.

The last week of school before winter break, Erik came running up Isabelle's front path with a large envelope. "It's from Jamie! Wait 'til you see what's inside." He opened the manila envelope and withdrew a couple of black and white photographs from between the sheaves of paper. Handing them to Isabelle, he said, "It's him—the boy in the scarf from the City."

Isabelle examined the pictures. "You two look adorable together."

"I know. I didn't even see Jamie taking these pictures. We were up on Coit Tower looking at the view. That's one of my best memories of San Francisco. Too bad it couldn't work out."

"Well, if you kept in touch, maybe you could hook up with him after high school. Then you'd be eighteen and he'd be twenty-two or three. Three or four years isn't that much of an age difference once you're older."

"A lot can happen in two years. Who knows where either of us will be at that point in our lives? Plus, I don't even have his phone number, know his last name, or where he lives."

"You're being very level-headed about this, Erik."

"I know. I still can dream about it, but it's pretty unlikely to come true." Erik took the pictures and placed them back into the envelope. "It's nice to hear from Jamie, though. I want you to meet Ryan. You'd love him."

"Hate to bring it up when you're so chipper, but how are you feeling about Jeremy?"

"I don't want to feel guilty, but I think I'm ready to move on," Erik admitted.

"Well those pictures sure verify that."

Erik grinned and put them back into the envelope. "Oh, I almost forgot—Merry Christmas." He handed her a small package.

"I thought we agreed on 'no gifts' this year."

"Just open it, Isabelle," Erik said. "I bought it in SF before we made that pact."

Isabelle turned the package over and untied the string. She held the small box in her hand and eased the lid off to reveal a rainbow necklace made of tiny beads nestled on a bed of cotton. "It's beautiful," she said, holding it up to the light. She placed it around her neck and fastened it in back. The beads hugged her throat. "It'll look great on me for our big debut."

"That's right. You're showing the video today. I can't believe you haven't even let me see it yet," Erik said.

"Nobody but Joshua and Mr. Martinez have seen it. I didn't even want to show it to him, but he wouldn't let me air it until I did."

"What do you think people are going to say?"

"God only knows. I think we'll get a variety of reactions, but that's good. At least everyone will be talking instead of being brain-dead as usual."

"You guys have been slaving away on this for weeks now, huh?"

"The video is just the icing on the cake. Maxine, genius that she is, uploaded a website for us. It's called whatsthecause.org and we've got all kinds of stuff on there that high school students can get involved with."

"That's awesome. I had no idea," Erik marveled.

"Well, we didn't really start off with that in mind, but it just kind of evolved the more we got involved."

"When do we get to see the video?"

"They're piping it through the TV in every classroom right after second period announcements. We decided to show all three segments back to back, so it's about a minute and a half long."

"I can't wait." Erik hugged Isabelle before heading off to his first period. "Good luck."

Isabelle sat through her own first period class watching the minutes on the clock tick by. She knew that they'd created something great but now, as the performance neared, she wondered, "Is Foresthill High ready for this?"

Isabelle wished that Mr. Kinney was her second period teacher so she could see his face as she unveiled her final project for the semester. Instead, she migrated toward her math class and settled in her seat just as the television screens across campus turned blue.

Mr. Martinez's voice came over the intercom: "Ladies and gentleman...we have a special version of the announcements today. Two of our sophomores have put together a series of dramatizations and we're going to air them here today. Watch with an open mind."

Isabelle pushed her tailbone back against her chair and waited for the opening shot. Across campus, students sat still as the first segment began.

On screen, the camera panned back from one individual's face to a group of six people standing in a circle holding various objects.

ii. Sticks and Stones

Individual: I am an Arab American.
Group: You are a terrorist. *(The group throws a fake hand grenade at his feet.)*
Individual: I am a Jewish person.
Group: You are a cheat. *(The group throws a Star of David at him.)*
Individual: I am a lesbian.
Group: You are a dyke. *(The group throws a Bible at her.)*
Individual: I am differently abled.
Group: You are useless. *(The group throws crutches at her.)*
Individual: I am a black man.

Group: You are a thug. *(The group throws a stocking cap at him.)*

Individual: I am a human being.

Group: You are who we say you are. *(They throw sticks and stones at her.)*

Individuals [in unison]: You cannot tell me that I am not me.

As the scene faded to black, it was replaced by the second segment. The circle now faced outward with the group linking arms together, singing and swaying back and forth. Every time an individual spoke, they let go of that person's hands and pushed him out of the circle and closed their ranks.

ii. Stones and Bones

Group: Our country 'tis of thee, great land of liberty...

Individual: Liberty for whom? Those who hold the power and wealth?

Group: O say, does that Star - Spangled Banner yet wave, o'er the land of the free and the home of the brave?

Individual: Isn't it true that nobody's free unless all of us are free?

Group: This land is your land, this land is my land. This land was made for you and me.

Individual: But weren't there already people living here when the Pilgrims arrived?

Group: God bless America, land that I love. Stand beside her and guide her through the night with the light from above.

Individual: Is God only on our side?

[Group disperses]

Individuals: [standing side by side]: Questions are patriotic. Keep asking them.

Murmurs of dissent followed the second scene, but were hushed by the curiosity of the larger group in anticipation of the final segment. Some people tittered when three people in pig costumes pranced onto the scene and began to chant:

iii. Sticks and Bricks

There once were three little pigs
Two were poor, but one was big
The wolf huffed and puffed
But they called his bluff,
And danced a little jig.

This is the song they sang
Across the valleys it rang:
You think you're the bomb
But you're really just wrong,
Just watch us get back with a bang.

The wolf the pigs did pursue,
Chasing him past the nice view.
He tripped on his feet
And into the street.
Where a truck arrived on cue.

The wolf scratched his throbbing head
And decided to go back to bed.
The moral is this
Watch who you dis'
Coz you might find yourself injured instead.

Now don't say this is a threat,
It's really only a bet,
If I were to guess
Or even confess,
We haven't seen the worst yet.

On a black background the credit roll ended with: "For more information on what you can do to foster tolerance in your community, go to www.whatsthecause.org." Isabelle held her breath as her classmates first whispered and then commented out loud.

"What the hell was that supposed to mean?"

"That was awesome. I'm checking out that website."

"Finally someone with brains has something to say."

"What crap! I can't believe someone had the nerve to put this together."

"Why don't they just go and join the terrorists!"

"I think it's great. People should be more aware."

"Aware of what? Other countries are just jealous of our freedom. That's what the President says."

"Then why are you disagreeing with someone's freedom to express what we just saw?"

"We're in a time of war. You can't just say stuff like this and divide the country."

"The country's already divided if you haven't noticed."

The comments resonated throughout the school in math classrooms to science labs and P.E. locker rooms. No one was short on opinions. Though Isabelle was rarely invisible at Foresthill High, today she experienced the impact that total recognition afforded. People who'd never smiled at her before gave her thumbs up signs as she passed by; others called her traitor and commie as she maneuvered through the lunchroom. Regardless of the reaction, Isabelle answered the same way every time: "Check out whatsthecause.org."

When sixth period rolled around, Isabelle made sure she was the first person in Mr. Kinney's classroom. Having heard unceasing opinions about her work all day long, she realized that the only person she really wanted to hear from was the teacher who'd provoked her to stage it.

Mr. Kinney met Isabelle at the door and extended his hand. She offered hers in return and waited for his critique.

"Well?" he said.

"Well," she answered.

"You know what you've done here?"

"I think so."

"Very well." He nodded. "Very well."

"Is that all?"

"You don't need me to tell you. The work says enough, doesn't it?"

"I'm not sure," Isabelle wavered.

"Just keep your eyes and ears open. You'll see what I mean," Mr. Kinney said.

"I was just hoping for a 'great job, Isabelle' from you," she confessed.

"The applause? The seductive applause?" Her teacher slapped his hands together sloppily. "Does that make it more worthwhile?"

"When you put it that way, I'm a little embarrassed."

"No need to be embarrassed. We all get sucked in by the applause. You reach success, not because someone else grants it to you, but because you've put your heart into it."

"I did put my heart and soul into it. I know I've never worked so hard on a school project before," she replied.

"Worth more than a silly 'A', isn't it?" Mr. Kinney remarked, and called the class to order. Throughout the period, students scrambled to pull together their projects before this afternoon's deadline. Content with the feeling in her heart, Isabelle sat in the corner, undisturbed by the bustle around her.

When Isabelle arrived home from school, she went online to update her blog on the video project. The page took longer to load than usual and, as she watched the graphics unfold, the counter in the corner caught her eye: 378 visitors. Just yesterday it had been 56. The home page appeared and she clicked on the Forum section where people could post their thoughts. Just yesterday, there were less than a dozen comments—half of which Isabelle had written herself; today there were well over a hundred. Without taking her eyes off of the screen, she reached for the phone.

"Maxine, go to the site. You're not going to believe it. IM me when you're online." Isabelle hung up and continued clicking on the posts that her classmates had submitted. She found comments on everything from each segment of the video, which people were analyzing in depth, to ideas that students were devising to promote acceptance. Some of the comments were scathing, but they were rebutted by Isabelle's growing fan club.

A pop-up chimed onto the screen. "We rock!"

"Right on! Isn't this the best?" Isabelle shot back.

"I never imagined," Maxine wrote.

"Check out all the posts. It's crazy!"

"K. Call u l8r."

Hours passed while Isabelle and Maxine devoured the comments on their site. As the evening wore on, new posts showed up as others added fuel to the conversations that had been started earlier in the day. Isabelle rubbed her eyes and moved her mouse to the corner of the screen; saturated with the commentary, she vowed to take a break until morning. Just at that moment, a new entry caught her eye. "Way to go, Isabelle!" it was titled. "Last one," she promised her tired eyes.

```
Isabelle—
Perhaps you remember me from my guest
lecture in Mr. Kinney's class earlier this
year? Mr. Kinney gave me a head's up about
your site and I streamed your video a few
minutes ago. I think you have some real
talent, not to mention a sophisticated grasp
on what's going on in the world today. I
wanted you to know that I'm a fan of your
work and hope you keep doing what you're
doing. If you're ever in LA, be sure to look
me up. I know you're going places, kiddo.
Just keep on being you!
-Meg O'Malley
```

Chapter Twenty-seven

For the next few weeks, Isabelle and Maxine enjoyed their newfound celebrity at Foresthill High. For better or for worse, they had become icons of free speech and drew attention wherever they went. By the time winter break rolled around, Maxine was glad to find reprieve from the fishbowl that had become their lives. The traffic to their website had slowed to a steady pace, but they'd gained a core following of teens across the country that were also dedicated to making their voices heard and their actions matter. Isabelle, the eternal extrovert, found her inbox full of messages every morning from students who wanted encouragement and advice.

On the first morning of vacation, Isabelle snuck out of bed and turned on the computer to check her email while Maxine was still asleep. After wading through a series of messages about her latest post on the merits of underground newspapers, she clicked on one with no title. "Isabelle—All I seek and cannot find is hidden in you. Wishing you the Merriest of Christmases. xo—M."

Maxine stirred and lifted her head from Isabelle's pillow. "Mm...What are you up to?"

Isabelle's mouse clicked on 'erase message' and she replied, "Email."

"You're obsessive. Get back over here."

"I know. It's your fault for teaching me how to use technology, though." Isabelle got up and pounced back on the bed.

"Oh, so I'm to blame?"

"Absolutely!" She tickled the bottom of Maxine's foot.

"I think you owe me something for cheating on me with your computer."

Isabelle stiffened. "Cheating? Don't say that word!"

"I can think of a way for you to make it up to me..."

"Ah, I love redemption."

"Here's the deal—you have to wear whatever I pick out for you for New Year's Eve," Maxine said.

"I reserve the right to veto," Isabelle replied. "But I'll let you choose what I try on, okay?"

"Conditional love." Maxine pretended to pout. "Where do you want to start?"

"How about some of those vintage clothing stores over in Lake Park?"

"Do you think their stuff will be nice enough?"

"Indulge me, okay? If we don't find anything then I'll go to the Mall without complaining," Isabelle replied.

Within an hour, Maxine and Isabelle were wandering the tree-lined main street of Lake Park. They waved a quick hello to Matthew and Joshua in Outbooks and wove their way through the head shops, novelty stores, and used clothing boutiques on Front St. Clattering through the tightly packed hangers that held antique dresses and vintage tuxedos, Maxine held up dress after dress in front of Isabelle, either nodding her head or wrinkling her nose.

"Getting ready for New Year's Eve?" Isabelle heard a Southern drawl behind her. She spun around and faced Reverend Kat.

Maxine said, "Hi there. Yeah, I can't believe it's only a few days away. We're super excited!"

Isabelle studied Rev. Kat's Saturday appearance with interest. "You're a lot shorter than I remember."

The Levi's wearing preacher replied, "I get that a lot. I just look tall when I'm in the pulpit and y'all are sitting."

"Sorry, I didn't mean it to be rude. It's just weird seeing you out here, in the world, you know."

Kat leaned in and whispered, "Don't tell anyone that I actually have a life, okay?" Then she leaned back and laughed. The girls couldn't help but join her.

Just then, a woman tapped on the glass of the store's front window. Kat said, "Oops, I always keep Delia waiting. Too much of a social butterfly, I guess." She smiled and touched Isabelle on the arm. "We'll get more of a chance to talk at the slumber party. Good luck finding an outfit!"

Isabelle watched the Reverend leave the store and turned to Maxine. "I can't believe how cool she is. It blows my mind."

"Is there anything in this store you want to try on?" Maxine prompted.

"Those, I guess." Isabelle pointed to the small pile Maxine had flung over her shoulder. "Then I think we should go somewhere else." She grabbed the stack of clothes and headed to the dressing room at the back of the store. Maxine stood outside the thin curtain waiting for Isabelle to emerge. Tempted to peek inside, Maxine urged Isabelle to hurry up. Four times Isabelle presented herself in a not-quite-so-right costume.

"None of these work," Maxine agreed. "Can I convince you to go to the Mall now?"

Isabelle puckered her mouth and squinted her eyes, but nodded in agreement. A half-hour bus ride delivered them in front of the Foresthill Mall. Inside, the place swarmed with teenagers with the purchasing power of their parents' credit cards in the days after Christmas.

"Ugh, I hate this place," Isabelle sneered.

"You promised me you'd have a good attitude, Bella. Come on—it'll be fun. We can ridicule the breeders," Maxine said. "Plus, remember why we're here—our first New Year's Eve together!"

"You're pretty excited about this, huh?"

"Maybe I should find another date, if you aren't..."

"Don't you dare! I'll be good," Isabelle conceded.

They strolled through the lower-level promenade, window-shopping and people watching. Neither Isabelle nor Maxine found anything that appealed to them.

"Let's check out Nordstrom's," Maxine said. "They might have something there."

They walked into the department store and rode the elevator to the top floor, where Brass Plum was located. Mostly winter coats and wool sweaters bedecked the racks and shelves, but they did find a small section of dresses and suits. Isabelle and Maxine decided that they would just pick out three things for each other to try on and then call it a day.

Swishing through the posh material, Isabelle heard a voice in the distance that raised the hairs on the back of her neck. "If I don't turn around, maybe it'll disappear," she coached herself.

Maxine, paying no attention to anything other than the black and lavender pinstriped suit that she was certain Isabelle would love, heard nothing. When she turned around to show Isabelle, she found herself face to face with Mandy Jenkins. She drew the suit to her chest and sucked in her breath. Maxine scanned the racks, but Isabelle was nowhere to be found.

"Hi," Mandy said. "Enjoying your vacation?"

"Yeah, it's been a nice break from school," Maxine answered. "How was Paris?"

"Fun. You know, I was just teasing Isabelle with that comment the day before break. I know she doesn't speak a word of French."

"I do, though." Maxine rested her hand on the rack in front of her and scooted the hangers back and forth. Her foot nudged at the metal bar holding up the circular rack while she tried to think of some way to get out of the conversation. Maxine almost jumped when her shoe hit something soft and it held on. She wriggled her foot out of Isabelle's grasp and stood upright.

"I found that out later. Sorry—I meant it as a joke."

"That's funny. No one laughed." Maxine's palm began to slide around the metal pole.

Mandy clasped her hands together in prayer mode. "Forgive me?"

"It doesn't really matter. Everything's cool now."

"Okay good. So, what are you shopping for?"

When Maxine held up the suit, Mandy said, "Oh, that's adorable. I bet it looks great on you."

"Oh it's not...I mean, I haven't tried it on yet."

"If you want an opinion, you can model it for me."

Isabelle seethed under the clothes rack. "What nerve!"

"Um, aren't your friends waiting for you?" Maxine asked, pointing to the group hanging out by the escalator.

"Not really. Come on, let me see it on you."

"I don't think that's a good idea. I can't afford it anyway," Maxine lied, and turned back to the rack.

"You and Isabelle hang out together a lot, huh?" Mandy made no signs of leaving as Maxine had hoped.

"Yeah. We're close."

"We used to be close, too," Mandy said. "But not anymore. I'm sure you know all about that..."

"I know enough, I guess. But she doesn't really talk about you."

"I don't suppose she would. Anyway, I hope you two are happy," Mandy said.

Maxine stared at Mandy and didn't respond.

"Wish her Happy New Year for me," Mandy added.

Maxine looked into Mandy's eyes and almost felt sorry for her. "I will."

"You know, I bet Isabelle would love that suit. You should get it for her."

A look of surprise fluttered across Maxine's face and she shifted her weight and landed on Isabelle's hand. She hopped away from the rack and prayed for Isabelle to stay quiet. Shrouded by the dark, Isabelle sucked on her injured fingers, feeling dizzy.

"Well, I guess I'll see you back at school," Mandy said, and walked back to her friends.

As soon as Mandy vanished down the escalator, Maxine peered through the dense clothing and pulled Isabelle out. "Whew! That was stressful," she declared. "We could have been caught."

"How do you think I felt with you stepping on me and her flirting with you? I almost busted out of there."

"I don't think she was flirting with me. It's pretty obvious she's still in love with you. Why else do you think she would come and talk to me?"

"I still don't like it," Isabelle sulked.

"Now you know how I feel."

"Let's just forget that Mandy Jenkins exists, okay?"

"Gladly. Now try this on. You do like *it*, don't you?" Maxine held the suit up against her chest. "Please?"

"Okay," Isabelle agreed. "But then can we go home? I think I've had enough shopping for one lifetime."

The suit fit Isabelle like it'd been made for her and they put an end to her shopping misery by buying it. Before she'd ducked under the clothes rack, Isabelle had laid out two dresses for Maxine to try on as well, but neither of them did Maxine's beauty justice.

"Don't worry about me," Maxine said. "I'll figure something out later."

"Let's hit the road. I need a nap," Isabelle said. She linked her arm through Maxine's elbow and steered her towards the exit.

Maxine spent most of the next morning at the Mall by herself. After the turmoil of buying Isabelle's suit, she knew better than to ask her for a return visit. By three o'clock, Maxine was not only frustrated, but also worried about not finding anything at all. Really wanting to get something special, something that would render Isabelle speechless, Maxine combed the stores for the perfect outfit.

Out of desperation, Maxine bought a gauzy white dress that looked nice against her brown skin. It wasn't stunning, but it would do, she decided. Once home, she modeled the dress for her parents.

"You look lovely," her mother said.

"What's wrong, honey?" her father asked.

"It's just that I wanted something more...unique, I guess," she said. "This is fine, but not earth shattering."

"Earth shattering?" her mother repeated. "What do you have in mind?"

"I have an idea." Her father disappeared up the stairs into the attic.

They heard him rustling around before emerging with a yellowing box. "You know what this is, don't you, Catherine?" he asked his wife.

"Oh Miko, I didn't know you still had that. Do you think it's appropriate?"

"Well, it'll look better on Maxine than it will in this old box, won't it?" he answered. He slit the tape holding the package together and pulled back the crackling tissue paper. Maxine saw a deep blue satin material rise up under her father's fingers. As he freed the dress from its confines, Maxine's eyes widened. Miko stood up and let the traditional Japanese dress unfold to the floor. "What do you think, baby?"

Maxine rose and reached out to touch the lightning blue material, letting her eyes roam over the hand-stitched embroidery of flaming red dragons with green scales and golden wings galloping over the canvas of the dress. "My God, it's fantastic. Unbelievable."

Her mother smiled. "Earth shattering?"

"Yes! Can I really?" she squealed, searching her father's eyes for permission.

"That's why I brought it out. I thought it might be what you were looking for." He dropped the dress into his daughter's hands and said, "Well, you better go try it on."

Maxine ran to her room and tore the gauzy gown over her head and slipped on the blue dress in one movement. She had to wiggle a little bit to get the form-fitting dress over her hips and then twirled around to face herself in the full-length mirror. Maxine held onto her long black hair and swirled it into a knot at the nape of her neck. Spotting a pair of chopsticks poking out of a pencil holder on her desk, Maxine stuck each one into one side of her bun and dropped her hands by her side. Tiny wisps of hair escaped the chopsticks and lingered on her neck. She said, "Isabelle Foxfire, you'll never know what hit you."

Chapter Twenty-eight

On the afternoon of December 31ˢᵗ, Maxine waltzed into the living room announcing, "Mom, I can't find my silver tear-drop earrings—do you know where..." Maxine stopped in mid-sentence. There stood her parents, Isabelle and Ana, all dumbstruck by Maxine's appearance.

"Oh my God," Isabelle said under her breath, but it sounded like a declaration to everyone in the room.

"Do you want us to pick them up tomorrow?" Catherine asked Ana.

"It's no problem. We live a lot closer than you do."

"You look stunning, Maxine. And Isabelle, you're looking pretty sharp yourself. I'm counting on you two to keep the boys off of each other, okay?" Miko instructed.

"You have my word, Mr. Kotamo," Isabelle agreed.

Maxine shot Isabelle a look and then hugged her father and mother. "Thank you so much for the dress."

The Kotamos waved their daughter off as she settled into the back seat of the Foxfire car. "You look gorgeous, Maxine," Erik, who had been waiting in the front seat, complimented her. "That's the most beautiful design."

"Thanks, Erik. You look pretty snazzy yourself."

Isabelle stroked the silky material clinging to Maxine's thigh and could barely wait to hold her in an embrace. "I must be the luckiest girl in the world," she whispered into Maxine's ear.

When Ana pulled into the church parking lot, she let the engine idle as she surveyed their surroundings. "If there's any sign of trouble, call me," she said, handing Isabelle her cell phone.

"Mom, don't stress out. It's just a party."

"It's them I'm worried about," Ana said, pointing to the small crowd gathered on the other side of the street. Isabelle strained to read the homemade signs stapled to sticks of wood: "Fornicators Go to Hell", "God Hates Fags", "God Made Adam & Eve, Not Adam & Steve."

"Oh man," Erik moaned. "I wasn't expecting this."

"What's wrong with those freaks?" Isabelle asked.

"That's probably what they're saying about us," Maxine said. "Come on, let's hurry up."

Ana turned off the engine and said, "I'm walking you in. Don't even argue, Isabelle."

Isabelle shut her open mouth and helped Maxine step out of the van. Reverend Kat stood at the church door with a serene look on her face as she watched the protestors across the street.

"My goodness, you three look fantastic. Wow!" Reverend Kat declared as they approached. "And you must be someone's mom?"

"Ana. Isabelle's mother."

"You're welcome to stay, if you want." She extended her arm towards the door.

"I just wanted to make sure they'd be safe," Ana said, motioning toward the anti-gay congregation who'd now begun chanting the slogans on their signs.

"Don't they make you mad?" Isabelle asked.

Rev. Kat smiled. "Mad? Oh, no. Sad, yes. I really feel sorry for them more than anything."

"What? They're a bunch of jerks," Isabelle stated.

"No, Isabelle. They're just misled and confused. We just need to help them understand that we're human, too."

"Uh oh, looks like someone's starting a sermon," an approaching voice said. They turned around and saw Delia arrive, flanked by two women in police uniforms. "Honey, wait until Sunday for that, okay? The kids are just here to have fun." The group broke into laughter, allowing everyone to tune out the rising voices across the street.

Ana released her children under the protection of the chaperones. "Go on inside. I'll pick you up in the morning," she said, as the kids edged towards the door.

The crew spent the next few hours decorating and setting up the social hall of the MCC church for the slumber party. The fourteen youth group members scrambled to lay down the new sleeping bags a sporting goods store had donated and filled them with hygiene kits and survival supplies. Once finished, the room was transformed into a cozy living room, complete with couches and a wide screen TV. Workers in the adjoining room were transforming the sanctuary into a disco.

"It's only six o'clock," Isabelle said. "We still have about two hours. What do you guys want to do?"

"How 'bout writing New Year's Resolutions that we can share with our visitors?" Jane suggested. "I think we should have some way of offering encouraging words without being preachy."

"Good idea," Isabelle agreed. "We can each write our own resolutions and paste them on the walls before the others get here."

Kat, overhearing Isabelle's direction, threw in her two cents. "I have some butcher paper in the basement—that might be fun to use. That way you can make it part of the decorations. Come on, Isabelle, you can help me carry the roll up here. Maxine, why don't you get the markers out of my office drawer," Kat instructed, throwing a set of keys in her direction.

Isabelle followed the Reverend down the steps into the church basement, enjoying the creaking of the old wood, breathing in the smell of damp stone. "Thanks again for letting us do this here," Isabelle said.

"As I said before, we're here to serve you. You kids are a much bigger blessing to us than we are to you."

"I still have a hard time believing that."

"Give and it shall be given unto you," Kat replied.

"You can just pull those out at any time, huh?"

"It's my job."

"Are you always this upbeat? I've never seen you have a bad day."

"Oh, I have my moments—just ask my wife. Wait—I take that back. Don't ask Delia, she might actually tell you."

At the end of the hallway, Kat grabbed the handle of the storage room door and found it locked. "Shoot. I forgot that I threw my keys to Maxine. Wait a sec and I'll run back up and get them from her," Kat said, and trotted back up the stairs.

Isabelle squatted next to the door and leaned her back against the cool wall. Closing her eyes, she said, "I want to be like Kat."

"Be like *you*," a voice inside her head replied.

Her eyes popped open and she peered down the hallway. She rubbed the goose bumps from her arms and asked, "Be like me? What's that supposed to mean?"

"Just keep on being you," the inner voice answered.

"I must be trippin'," Isabelle said.

"You okay down here?" Kat called from the stairwell. "Sorry—it took me a few minutes to find Maxine." When she approached, she observed the pallor of Isabelle's face and repeated her question.

"This place is bizarre. I'm hearing voices."

"Good ones or bad ones?" Kat asked.

"Good, I guess. Am I crazy?"

"Nah, just open."

"It's kinda freaky."

"Don't worry about it. Maybe you'll be the next Joan of Arc," Kat teased.

"Didn't she get burned at the stake for hearing voices?"

"Right. Bad example. I'm just saying that it's okay to listen to intuition."

"If you say so."

"Hey, let's get this paper upstairs—the guests will be here soon."

With each of them on an end, Isabelle and Kat carried the roll to the Rec room and plopped it down on a cafeteria-length table and unfurled a long strip of paper. While they were downstairs, the others had decided to make the individual resolutions into a group mural, where everyone would write down their affirmations together. Geared with felt tip markers, each person copied the statements they'd written onto the poster. When the last person finished his inscription, two people got on each end of the paper and held it to the wall while Maxine taped it.

Everyone crowded around the poster reading the resolutions and complimenting each other's contributions, when the first knock landed on the outer doors. All faces turned towards the sound, but nobody moved. "Come on, welcome committee." Jane spurred them into action. "Let's greet our first arrivals."

Chapter Twenty-nine

The visitors arrived in pairs and trios throughout the next hour, some having decided to show up without hesitation, others needing more coaxing. By nine o'clock, Erik counted nineteen people who'd responded to the invitation. Almost all of the faces were familiar to them; the outreach they'd been doing for the past six weeks had paid off. Isabelle and Maxine introduced everyone by name and helped bridge the initial apprehension between the guests and hosts. Within an hour, however, one couldn't tell which was which.

The congregation had spent the majority of the afternoon transforming the place of worship into a place of enchantment. Silver and blue streamers strung from the rafters cascaded into crepe waterfalls over doorways. Helium balloons floated on their free will, bobbing across the floor like wayward dancers.

For the first few minutes, the girls stood close to the wall, soaking in the atmosphere, not quite believing what they'd created.

Isabelle put her hand in Maxine's. "Wanna dance?"

"Nobody else is out there, yet," Maxine observed. A few boys near the stage were dancing in place, but everyone else was planted in chairs or on couches in the adjoining room.

"Well, I guess that means we have to be brave, huh?"

"I think I forgot to tell you, but I don't really know how to dance. Actually, I've never even been to a dance before," Maxine admitted.

"You're kidding me? You've been so excited about this night and you've never danced before?"

"I know. It sounds crazy. But I'm willing to learn." Maxine batted her eyelashes at Isabelle.

"Good thing my dad taught me how to lead." Isabelle took Maxine by the hand and led her about ten feet away from the wall. Placing one hand on her hip and the other in Maxine's hand, Isabelle taught Maxine how to do a slow waltz. At first they stumbled and laughed over each other's awkwardness, but they soon became role models for other couples who'd never been schooled in dance etiquette.

Noticing that others were copying them, Isabelle called out, "Come on, everyone. Follow us." She spun Maxine into the middle of the floor and started counting, "One, two, three....one, two, three." Other pairs drifted into the circle and the band followed suit by playing some oldies.

Soon the dance floor contained more people than the walls, and New Year's Eve had finally begun. Even when Isabelle and Maxine stopped to rest, others remained, improvising on Isabelle's basic waltz and then easing into modern dance moves. Dropping into a chair, Isabelle pulled Maxine onto her lap. "This is the best night of my life. Thanks for being here with me."

"I love you," Maxine returned. "No one else could take your place."

"Have I told you how beautiful you look tonight?"

"Not enough," Maxine said.

"I never want this moment to end," Isabelle proclaimed. "I'm happier than I've ever been before."

Maxine sighed and leaned back into Isabelle's embrace. They melted into each other as they watched the other teens dancing and playing as if residing in some kind of gaytopia.

About ten o'clock a solitary knock tapped on the door. Isabelle barely heard it through the laughter and conversation filling the room. She looked at Maxine. "Was that the door? Come with me."

They walked into the foyer. "Is someone there?"

"Yes," a muffled voice answered. "Is it too late or can I still join you?"

Isabelle opened the door and saw a young man with a scarf wrapped around his neck and mouth and a stocking cap pulled down over his ears. "Come on in. Glad you could make it." She looked into his eyes trying to figure out if she knew this one or not, as she led him into the Rec hall.

Erik looked up from his conversation with Anthony and Giselle when the stranger entered the room. He stared at the young man whose face was nearly covered, but recognized him, nonetheless. It appeared to Erik that the boy was actually looking for him, because when they locked eyes, he detected a smile lift the edges of the scarf. Erik said, "Excuse me a second," and walked over to the doorway where Isabelle and Maxine stood.

"Hi," he said. "What a surprise to see *you* here."

The boy replied, "Well, it took about all the guts I had to show up tonight. I saw one of the flyers your group put up a few weeks ago but I didn't imagine I'd actually come. I had to come up with all kinds of excuses for the guys as to why I wasn't going out to party with them."

220

"Well, I'm glad you did, Mark," Erik said. "It's great to see you."

The girls exchanged raised eyebrows and stifled smiles. "Welcome Mark. Come on in and join the party," Maxine said.

Isabelle whispered, "I guess turned out to be a lesbian after all," and Maxine socked her in the arm.

Mark hesitated and didn't move from the doorway. Erik said, "We'll just hang out here for a few minutes while he gets used to the place." He led Mark back into the hallway and sat him down on the steps into the sanctuary. Mark loosened the scarf and took off his hat.

"I don't really know if I am or not, but I know that I don't feel the same way the other guys do. I can shut off my feelings and just go along with the group, but then something happens that makes me know that I'm different," Mark explained.

Erik listened for awhile without speaking. He put his arm around Mark's shoulders. "Is this okay?" he asked.

"I don't know. Yes and no."

Erik lifted his arm and gave Mark some distance. "Hey, you don't have to know right now. It's a process. But I want you to know that I can empathize. I'm not always comfortable or clear about what I want or need, either."

"How do you deal with it on a daily basis?"

"Well, the only thing that really gets me through is having such great friends. I'm totally closeted at home, but I've got people here to lean on the rest of the time."

"You're lucky."

"What I have you can have, too," Erik offered. "Hey, you're here. That's a great first step to getting support."

"The only reason I actually had the courage to knock on that door was because I guessed that you'd be here. If you weren't, I was going to just walk back out, pretending I'd come to the wrong place," he admitted.

"Well, I, for one, am glad you stayed," Erik stated. "I think you'll find that everyone here is open and friendly. Some may look a little scary, but they're just wearing a different disguise than you are. It's all the same, though."

Mark played with the edges of his scarf, which he'd unraveled during their conversation. "I don't know if I can go in there, Erik."

"Then I'll just have to pull a sleeping bag into the hallway and stay out here with you."

"Why are you always so nice to me, even when I was a jerk to you?"

"Well, I believe in second chances." Erik stood up and held his hands out to Mark who allowed himself to be pulled up. They stood face to face, holding hands for a few seconds before walking into the main room where much of the party had settled into watching the movie *But I'm a Cheerleader*. Erik plumped an oversized beanbag and pushed Mark into it. He then grabbed a plate from the buffet line, filled it up, and delivered it to Mark before sitting down next to him.

"Is this okay?" Erik asked again. This time Mark just smiled and nodded, allowing the edge of Erik's thigh to touch his own throughout the duration of the film.

When the movie was over, Jane called out, "Fifteen minutes 'til New Year's! Okay, we're going to read our resolutions aloud before the clock strikes midnight."

They linked hands in front of the poster and declared their intentions for the New Year. When it was Isabelle's turn, she read, "I will treat each day as if it's a new year, full of possibilities and opportunities for growth."

Maxine followed: "I will stand up to people who say hateful things and fight discrimination in all of its forms."

Erik read, "I will take off the masks and be myself." He squeezed Mark's hand as the group read their resolutions.

Jane, the timekeeper, then declared that the midnight hour was upon them. "Let's go into the sanctuary and make some noise," she yelled.

The thirty some-odd people tripped and stumbled over each other to get into the sanctuary before the church bell tolled. A few jumped up onto the altar and grabbed tambourines and maracas. Delia pulled her guitar over her shoulder and strummed a few notes while Kat seized a pair of sticks and sat behind the drum set. Isabelle hugged Maxine from behind, while Mark stood close to Erik. Todd held his watch up in the air and began to count down the last ten seconds of 2001. Their rising energy filled the sanctuary with a buzz.

"Three, two, one!" Todd chanted and the place erupted into celebration. People banged on instruments, danced, and shouted out New Year's greetings. They rejoiced in the newness of a year yet unspoiled by disappointments, heartache, and despair.

Mark and Erik spun in circles until they ended up in a pile on the floor. "Happy New Year," Erik said. He lay flopped across Mark's stomach, his head still dizzy from the dance. "Aren't you glad you came?"

Still trying to catch his breath, Mark answered by pulling Erik into an embrace. Their hearts thumping against each other's chests, Erik soaked in the scent of Mark's soap that had captivated his senses in the truck that night after the Homecoming party.

"Well, would ya look at that," Isabelle said, after she'd finishing dousing Maxine in New Year's kisses. She pointed to the boys wrapped together across the room. "Do you think they'll kiss?"

Maxine turned Isabelle's face back to hers. "Get out of Erik's business, nosy!"

"What fun would that be?" Isabelle pouted.

Her attention back on her girlfriend, Isabelle not only missed Erik's lips meeting Mark's for the first time, but also a pair of green eyes peering through a stained glass window outside.

Frosty eyelashes blinked against frozen cheeks. Leaving a cold handprint on the window, their owner stepped out into the first few minutes of 2002 and let a solitary "Happy New Year" ring onto the street.

Inside, Isabelle shook her head to dislodge the voice she thought she was imagining. Her eyes drifted and locked onto the spot where the handprint remained.

Maxine tugged at Isabelle's sleeve. "Come on, everyone's claiming sleeping bags—I want to get one next to yours."

"Be there in a sec. Just save me a space," Isabelle replied, without breaking her gaze.

As Maxine exited, Isabelle walked over to the door near the smudged window. She peered outside and listened. Nothing but a stray newspaper danced down the street. Isabelle puffed hot breath onto a green panel of the stained glass window and wrote, "Happy New Year" with a gloved finger in the steam.

Stepping back inside, Isabelle skipped into the Rec hall singing off-tune. "It's a boot-i-ful day in the gayborhood, a boot-i-ful day for a gaybor." She tripped over the extension cord running the TV and flopped into Maxine's arms. "Won't you be my gaybor?"

Sneak Preview from

Erik & Isabelle
Junior Year at Foresthill High

Since Isabelle had avoided fulfilling her P.E. requirements until she was a junior, she now had to face one more semester of the hated subject. She entered the locker room and sat down on the bench in front of her P.E. locker. Unlocking the combination, Isabelle pulled out a P.E. uniform that had been marinating in the cramped space for a two-week vacation. Wrinkling her nose, she waved the uniform in the open air and kicked off her shoes. When the one-minute warning bell rang, Isabelle slid her legs into the shorts and swept the t-shirt over her head.

She ran with untied tennis shoes into the gym, squeaking the rubber purposely on the slick floor and landing on her P.E. number right before Ms. Kruder took roll. Unlike her other classes, Isabelle made sure that she was always on time for roll call. The stragglers were immediately instructed to run laps around the gym until she was done with attendance. Very few people were late twice to Ms. Kruder's class.

Isabelle surveyed her neighboring numbers, looking over the heads of the freshmen and sophomores surrounding her. Most of them shuffled their feet, none too pleased to be part of this cattle call. When Isabelle turned completely around, her eyes landed on a familiar but almost-forgotten face. Isabelle swiveled back to the front and muttered, "Just my luck."

As they were doing their warm-ups, Isabelle tried not to be distracted by Mandy. It had been almost two years since they'd broken up, and the initial sting of betrayal had subsided into mild agitation.

Ms. Kruder announced that they would start this semester off with badminton. Isabelle sighed. "Thank God. Something that requires little effort."

"Since we'll be playing doubles, you'll need to select a partner," Ms. Kruder directed.

Isabelle scanned the gym, looking for someone to join up with. Just as she was approaching a lost looking 9th grader, someone else grabbed the girl's arm and linked it with hers. Everywhere Isabelle turned, pairs stood side by side, giggling with relief. Isabelle approached Ms. Kruder and said, "I don't mind playing by myself against doubles. I think everyone's partnered already."

Ms. Kruder belted out, "If anyone does *not* have a partner, raise your hand!"

Isabelle saw Mandy lift her hand and give a feeble wave. Isabelle briefly considered failing P.E. in order to avoid this partnership, but then realized she'd have to take it over as a senior.

Taking a deep breath Isabelle walked over to Mandy and said, "Oh well, I guess we're stuck together."

Mandy smiled. "Glad you're so thrilled about it."

"Are you?" Isabelle retorted.

"Hey, I have no hard feelings towards you, Isabelle. You're the one who can't stand the sight of me."

"That's not necessarily true," Isabelle stammered.

"Then this should be fun," Mandy said. "Grab a racket and come on."

Isabelle said, "What are you doing in P.E. anyway? You should be done with this by now."

"Oh, I'm just taking it for elective credits. I don't really need it, but it keeps me limber for cheerleading."

Isabelle grimaced and muttered, "One more reason we weren't meant to be."

"What's that? I couldn't quite catch it."

"Oh nothing, just talking to myself."

"Let's find some younguns to duel." Mandy refused to let Isabelle's snide comments damper her spirits. She skipped towards an empty court and bounced the birdie on her racket until Isabelle took a place beside her. "Do you know how to play?" Mandy asked.

"How hard can it be?" Isabelle questioned. "You just hit that little thingy back and forth over the net, right?"

"Pretty much. It can get competitive, though."

Another pair answered their call for a match and Isabelle found herself enjoying the volleying back and forth of the birdie. Though she and Mandy may not have been meant to be as a couple, they sure flowed together on the court. As Ms. Kruder blew the whistle, Mandy and Isabelle were both reaching for the same shot flying over the net. Colliding mid-air, they toppled to the ground, entangling their rackets, arms, and legs in a twisted mess. Lying together in a heap Isabelle said, "Are you okay?"

Mandy groaned, "I think so. Are you?" She felt Isabelle's weight on top of her and shivered. It had been so long since she'd felt Isabelle's body against hers and, despite the throbbing pain in her ankle, she wanted to remain there for just a moment longer.

"What is it about my presence that makes you want to fall on the ground? Remember last year?" Isabelle shifted and released the pressure from Mandy's leg. "You make a nice cushion."

Composing a pained grin, Mandy replied, "Glad I could accommodate you. See, I told you this would be fun."

"I feel great." Isabelle popped onto her feet and stretched her arms into the air. Realizing that Mandy wasn't moving, she said, "Hey, you're actually injured." She reached her hands down and lifted Mandy up.

"I'll be fine. It's nothing worse than what I usually experience during cheerleading." Mandy gingerly put her foot onto the floor and began limping to the locker room.

"Wait, let me help you." Isabelle put her arm around Mandy's back and acted as a crutch across the gym. "Ms. Kruder—Mandy's going to need some ice for her ankle," she called over to her teacher.

Ms. Kruder jogged over to her office, rustled in the freezer for an ice pack, and brought it into the locker room. She found the girls sitting on a bench together and asked, "What happened?"

"Oh, we just had a minor fender-bender," Mandy explained. "It's not a big deal." She then looked at the purplish hue coloring her ankle and frowned.

"It looks terrible," Isabelle said. "You should go to the hospital and get X-rayed."

"If it doesn't feel better in a couple of hours, I'll go after school."

Ms. Kruder looked at the ankle critically. "Well, my vote is to send you to Emergency right away. I'm going to call your parents."

The bell rang and the locker room emptied. Isabelle stayed next to Mandy and waited to hear from Ms. Kruder. "I'm really sorry," Isabelle said. "Does it hurt a lot?"

"It's not your fault. We both got caught up in the competition," Mandy said. "I just hope it doesn't end up being fractured."

"I would just feel terrible if it was," Isabelle said. "Then you wouldn't be able to cheerlead."

Mandy replied, "Let's just wait and see. No point in getting upset about what's already happened. Shouldn't you be getting to third period?"

A new set of students began filling up the locker room. "I guess I better get changed." Isabelle stood up. "Will you call me and let me know what the doctor says?"

"Yeah, I'll let you know," Mandy said. "Same number?"

Isabelle could tell by the tight expression on Mandy's face that the pain was getting more intense. "Why don't I just wait here with you until you're ready to go—I'm late already, so what's a few more minutes?" Isabelle sat back down close to Mandy and put a hand on her back.

Mandy closed her eyes and let the warmth of Isabelle's hand penetrate through her t-shirt and override the ache creeping up her leg. "Thanks Isabelle, I'd forgotten what a good friend you are. I miss our friendship."

Isabelle hesitated before responding. Unsure whether she was betraying Maxine, she lifted her hand and set it on her own thigh. "It's been a long time."

"Do you ever think about me? Miss me?" Mandy murmured, her eyes growing sleepy.

Isabelle shook her shoulder lightly. "Don't zone out, Mandy. You need to stay alert until help arrives." Her words accompanied the entrance of two paramedics.

Ms. Kruder helped them load Mandy onto a stretcher. "Your parents are going to meet you at the hospital. I'll call you at home tonight to see how you're doing."

Mandy lay her head down on the pillow and allowed them to carry her out of the locker room. Her eyes, however, didn't leave Isabelle's face. Isabelle lifted her hand and waved, mulling over what was taking place between them. Shaking her head, as if to empty it of unwanted thoughts, Isabelle got dressed and asked Ms. Kruder for a pass to U.S. History.

About the Author

After witnessing the disenfranchisement of gay and lesbian teenagers, English teacher, Kim Wallace was inspired to write a four-book series that would embrace the lives of a typically invisible and misunderstood population. *Erik & Isabelle* bloomed out of a desire to reach a group of young people in need of connection and understanding. Kim Wallace earned her Bachelor of Arts in History at UC Santa Barbara, Master's Degree in Education at UCLA, and Educational Administration credential at Sacramento State. Currently, Kim works in the public schools as a curriculum and instruction coach.

<u>Contact</u>: Kim Wallace is available for appearances and presentations to groups of all sizes. For scheduling information, email: info@foglightpress.com or call 916-879-6645.